59

PIECES OF
THE PAST

PATCHWORK MYSTERIES

PIECES OF THE PAST

SUSAN PAGE DAVIS

Guideposts
New York, New York

www.guideposts.com
(800) 932-2145
Guideposts Books & Inspirational Media

Cover design by Wendy Bass
Cover illustration by Joyce Patti
Interior design by Lorie Pagnozzi
Typeset by Aptara

Printed and bound in the United States of America
10 9 8 7 6 5 4 3 2 1

Family Patterns
Time to Share
Muslin Mystery
Timeless Treasures
Homespun Holiday
Pieces of the Past

PIECES OF
THE PAST

CHAPTER ONE

Sarah Hart got out of her silver Grand Prix and pulled a large bundle wrapped in a plastic trash bag from the backseat. The Bradford Manor Nursing Home grounds were blanketed in shimmering snow, but the parking lot and driveway had been plowed down to the bare pavement. The distant Berkshire Mountains glistened white, with purple and gray shadows on their snowy slopes and swaths of dark evergreens among the bare hardwood trees. The view satisfied something in Sarah's artistic soul, as her breath formed white vapor clouds in the air. She hefted the soft package and shoved the car door shut.

She entered the lobby, stopping briefly at the front desk to say hello to Grace, one of the nurses. A moment later, she tapped softly on her father's half-open door. From inside his room, she heard him talking with another man.

"We had an awful time in Italy," her father said. "I was at Salerno."

"That was a tough battle."

"Sure was. Fiats zooming in low over us and strafing the ground. I thought we'd never get out of there."

"I hear ya. The fight in the Pacific was half a world away from Italy, but there was more than once when I thought we'd never get out of that jungle."

"Hello, Dad!" Sarah entered the sunny room and smiled at him and the man he regaled with his battle tales. "Hello. I'm William's daughter, Sarah."

The gray-haired man in the wheelchair quickly tucked something into his pocket and looked up at her. He nodded and smiled, his brown eyes sweeping her face. "Vern Pickett. I'm down the hall. William and I were just swapping war stories."

William had served in the European theater in the 1940s.

"Those Italians were lousy shots, or I wouldn't be here," William said.

He didn't talk about it often. In fact, he didn't talk so passionately about much of anything these days. She laid the garbage bag she carried on her father's bed.

"Are you a veteran, Mr. Pickett?" she asked as she unzipped her down parka.

"Yes, ma'am. I joined my state National Guard infantry unit in nineteen forty-two, but we became part of the Americal Division, in the Pacific, under Major General Alexander Patch."

William squinted at Vern. "What did you say your name was again?"

"Vern Pickett."

William nodded, though he might not remember the name five minutes from now. His eyelids drifted shut, and Sarah stepped closer to his chair.

"Dad, I brought your present over. I'm sorry I didn't have it quite finished on your birthday yesterday."

"What?" He blinked and focused on her. "What's that?"

"I brought the quilt I made you. It's finished now." She turned and slipped the garbage bag off the gift and took the quilt in her arms. She unfolded one end and draped it over her father's lap. "There, see? I finished the stitching last night. Would you like me to put it on the bed for you?"

William nodded and ran his fingertips over one of the squares. His lips curved into a slight smile. She and Jason and Maggie and the twins had come on his birthday to tell him how much they loved him.

"You made that?" Vern asked. "That's some fine work. Looks nice and warm."

Sarah unfolded more of the quilt. She placed one edge in his hand. "Thank you. I hoped it would help since Dad gets cold, even when the heat's up. I used a few of his old flannel shirts to make most of the squares for this."

"That's a great idea." Vern fingered the soft plaid material. "I'm sure he'll use that all the time."

"I hope it gives him good memories and pleasant dreams," Sarah said.

Vern looked over at William. "So, you just had a birthday, eh?"

But William was silent, his hands caressing the edges of the quilt.

Sarah and Vern exchanged a knowing look.

"How old is he?" Vern asked.

"Ninety-seven."

Vern whistled softly. "He seemed pretty alert today."

"I'm glad you caught him at a good time."

Vern nodded. "Well, I suppose I'd better head on down the hall. Nice to meet you." He groped for the brakes on his wheelchair's side, then bent over the armrest, trying to see it.

"Let me help you."

As Sarah stepped to his side, Vern shifted and a small square photograph fell from his shirt pocket, landing face up on the carpet. Sarah picked it up.

She glanced at it as she held it out to him. A young woman smiled softly at whomever had taken the picture, the life in her eyes shining clearly from the black-and-white wallet-size picture.

"Oh. Thanks." Vern took it and stuck it into his pocket.

Sarah released the brake on his wheelchair. "She's striking. It that a picture of your wife?"

He hesitated, not meeting her gaze. "No. She . . . her name was Alice."

"She's very pretty. That picture looks as though you've been hanging on to it for a while."

"Oh, yes." He smiled then. "Been carrying that for a long time. It went to Guadalcanal with me."

"She must be special."

"Well...yes."

Sarah remained silent and waited. Something about the yellowed picture made Vern uncomfortable.

He gave a halfhearted shrug. "I haven't spoken with her in years."

"You lost touch?" Sarah asked.

"Something like that. After the war, I tried to find her, but...well, some things just don't work out."

"Do you want to tell me about it?"

He squeezed up his lips for a moment. "Not much to tell now. It's been over sixty years."

"Have you tried looking for her recently? You know, with the Internet, a lot of people have success in locating old friends."

"I tried a little bit, but I'm not exactly a whiz with those computers."

Sarah nodded.

A tall young man in jeans and a Red Sox sweatshirt appeared in the doorway. "Hey, Grandpa! I've been looking for you. Thought you were AWOL."

Vern chuckled and looked at Sarah. "My grandson Scott." He began to turn his wheelchair toward the door. "I met one of my neighbors and got talking. You know how that goes."

Scott stepped into the room and smiled at Sarah. "Hi." His warm brown eyes matched Vern's, but Scott's held a friendly twinkle his grandfather seemed to have lost.

"Hello." Sarah stood. "I'm Sarah Hart, William's daughter."

Her father opened his eyes and blinked. "Who's that young man?"

"He's Vern's grandson, Dad."

"Who?"

She drew his attention to Vern. "Your friend Vern's grandson."

"Is that right? How are you, son?"

Scott nodded at him. "Just came to find Grandpa for a game of checkers."

"You should see what Mrs. Hart made for her dad." Vern said to him.

"Oh?"

Sarah stood and gestured to her father's bed. "He's talking about this quilt. I made it for my father's birthday."

Scott surveyed the quilt, which Sarah had refolded and placed at the foot of the bed. "That's really nice. My wife likes to sew, too, but she hasn't done much lately."

"Sarah's always sewing something," William said. "Quilts are a specialty of hers."

"Know what's extraspecial about it?" Vern asked.

Scott looked down at him, a ready smile playing at his lips. "Why don't you tell me?"

"She made it out of William's old shirts."

Scott blinked and glanced at Sarah. "Really? That *is* interesting."

Sarah laughed. "Dad had several older flannel shirts that he liked, but they were getting thin on the elbows. I decided to put pieces of them into the quilt top. He can enjoy their colors, and they'll still keep him nice and warm."

Scott stepped over to the bed and fingered one of the red plaid squares that still held a pocket with a buttoned flap. "That's a very thoughtful gift."

"Thank you."

Scott positioned himself behind Vern's chair. "You ready to go down to the lounge and get beat at checkers?"

"Ha! We'll see about that." Vern lifted a hand in farewell. "Nice talking to you, William. And nice to meet you, Mrs. Hart."

"It's Sarah."

Sarah smiled as she watched them leave. Scott guided the wheelchair carefully through the doorway, all the time keeping up a cheerful interplay with his grandfather.

"Nice young man." She swung around toward her father again.

"You could help him find her," he said.

"Oh, you heard all that? I don't know, Dad."

"It's a terrible thing to lose someone you care about."

William's mother had disappeared when he was a young boy. He knew what it was like to lose someone close. He'd lived his whole life that way.

Sarah spread the flannel quilt on her father's bed and smoothed it down. When she'd finished, she looked over at him. He sat leaning back in his recliner, his eyes closed, and he gave a soft snore. Zipping her parka, she walked into the hall and closed the door.

As she entered the sitting room at the front of the nursing home, Scott Pickett was crossing the room carrying some packets of sugar. On a small table over near the aviary, Vern was setting up a checkerboard next to two large mugs that sat on the table.

Scott paused when he saw her. "Mrs. Hart, it was nice to meet you and your father. Thanks for talking to my grandpa."

"I enjoyed it. Sometimes my dad is a little fuzzy on conversation, but your grandfather seems sharp as a tack."

"Oh, he is. He's only here because he took a fall a few weeks ago."

"I'm sorry to hear that. Was he injured badly?"

"Cracked his tibia. That's why he's in the wheelchair. His shoulder was kind of messed up, too, and he had a lot of bruises. He stayed in the hospital a few days, then went to rehab for two weeks, but he was still weak. The doctor felt he ought to go into a skilled care home, where he could have supervision and therapy."

Sarah nodded. "Sometimes that's best, especially for older people who live alone."

Scott hesitated for a moment. "That quilt you made your father—Grandpa's right. It's very special."

"Thanks. I think he'll enjoy it."

"I wondered…do you sew for other people?"

"I've been known to make quilts for folks outside the family." She thought she knew what was coming.

"My wife, McKenna, doesn't sew much since she had our little boy. He keeps her hopping. But…well, I wondered how much it would cost for a quilt like that for Grandpa. He's got a closet full of flannel shirts, and he only wears a few now. He seemed to really like the quilt, and it would mean a lot to him. Like you said, it's useful, but at the same time, it's…"

"Full of memories?" Sarah suggested.

"Exactly."

She nodded. "I like you, Scott, and I like your grandfather. I'd be happy to work on a quilt for him. My father's is machine stitched, so it didn't take all that long."

His sunny grin broke out. "Terrific. I'll pay you, of course."

Sarah patted his arm. "Just bring me a few of his old flannel shirts." She opened her purse. "Let me give you a card with my address on it. Do you live here in Maple Hill?"

"Yes, ma'am."

She handed him one of her business cards. "Just give me a call when you're ready to bring them over. I have some scraps left from Dad's in case I need to fill in a little."

"Don't you need more than that?"

She shrugged. "I'll pick up some batting and a flannel sheet for the backing, but I'll wait until I see what colors you bring me before I think about that."

"Thank you very much." Scott slipped the card into his pocket.

He walked with her to the door and reached to open it for her.

Another thought popped into Sarah's mind. "Scott…"

He paused with his hand on the doorknob. "Yeah?"

"That picture your grandfather carries around with him—the woman named Alice. Has he ever shown that to you before?"

"Many times." Scott sighed. "Don't tell me he dragged that out and made you look at it."

"No, it was accidental. It fell on the floor and…I just wondered who she is."

Scott shrugged. "We'd never heard of her until after Grandma died a couple of years ago. But since then, it's come up a lot. Alice. Apparently she was his girl before the war."

"He said he couldn't find her after the war ended."

"I'm not sure how hard he looked. I mean, he and Grandma were married in nineteen forty-seven, and they were very happy together, so he couldn't have been too heartbroken, could he?"

Sarah considered that. It certainly was easy to become nostalgic as time passed. After her husband Gerry passed away, she had spent many hours thinking about "the good old days."

Scott glanced over to where Vern waited, watching them across the large, sunny room. "Hey, I'd better get over there. It just bothers me a little that he talks about Alice Ward more now than he does about Grandma." He flashed a smile. "Anyway, thanks for talking to him. I'm sure he gets lonesome."

"It was my pleasure. And you bring me those shirts, all right?" Sarah touched his sleeve. "Keep taking good care of your grandfather. I know how stressful that can be, especially when they drift off into the past. I'll enjoy making the quilt for him."

Sarah went out into the cold air. The sun was setting behind the hills to the west. She got into the car and headed for town, thinking about her family and Scott's. She hadn't thought she'd wind up this way—widowed, and with her father spending his last years in a nursing home. She'd always thought she and her husband Gerry would age together and enjoy this part of their lives as a couple. But Gerry had been gone five years now. She had her children and grandchildren, and she had dear friends and interests that kept her busy, but she missed Gerry terribly.

Her father knew what it was like. "It's a terrible thing to lose someone you care about." Sarah could reunite two people torn apart by war over fifty years ago. It was worth a shot.

CHAPTER TWO

The next morning after breakfast, Sarah decided to get a stew going in the slow cooker for dinner that night. As she peeled the carrots, her boarder, Belle Silver, came into the kitchen and set her backpack on a chair.

"Good morning. That looks like the promise of a delicious supper."

"Hi." Sarah smiled. Belle had the gift of being cheerful, even early in the morning. "I'll be shopping later. Anything you want me to pick up for you at the store?"

"I can't think of anything special." Belle opened the refrigerator and took out a container of low-fat yogurt.

"The weather report says Maple Hill is due for a heavy snowfall this weekend. I figured I'd better lay in some extra supplies and batteries."

"Sounds good," Belle said. "Maybe bring me some more yogurt?"

"Sure thing." Sarah put the lid on the cooker and bundled up the vegetable peels. "I plan to get my errands out of the way so I can hole up and quilt through the storm."

Belle chuckled. "I'll be right there with you, with a cross-word book in my hand." As different as they were, Sarah and her young boarder were becoming good friends, especially after Sarah had recently helped Belle and her brother by solving a mystery this past Christmas. The episode had made the holidays extra-exciting, and Sarah was glad things had now slowed to a less frantic pace.

After Belle left for work, Sarah hummed a favorite hymn as she ran the vacuum around the floors of wide pine boards in the dining room and living room. As she put the vacuum cleaner away, she heard a ringing from the back of the house. She hurried into the kitchen to grab the cordless phone.

"Sarah, this is Pastor John. I'm looking for someone who can fill in for Angela Miller's Sunday school class this week."

"I'd be happy to do it," she said.

Pastor John chuckled. "Thank you so much, Sarah. I knew you wouldn't mind."

"Of course," Sarah said, though it meant giving up some of her quilting time. "Does Angela have the teacher's materials at home?"

"She just dropped them off here at church. I could bring them to you. ..."

"I'll come get them a little later, since I'm going shopping anyway," Sarah said.

"Fantastic. I'll be at the church studying this morning. Come any time."

Sarah quickly closed the closet on the vacuum and straightened the magazines on the coffee table. She sat down with a notepad and jotted a few items for her shopping list. Maybe she'd have time to stop at Wild Goose Chase, her friend Vanessa's fabric and yarn shop. It was possibly Sarah's favorite store in Maple Hill, and she used any excuse to stop in and browse. This time she'd have a mission to fulfill.

She was about to put on her jacket when the phone rang again.

"Sarah, this is Scott Pickett. I'm heading for work, but I wondered if it would be okay for my wife to drop off the shirts we talked about for the quilt?"

"Certainly," Sarah said, "but if it's easier for her, I can swing by and get them. I'm going out anyway this morning."

"Are you sure you don't mind?"

"Not at all."

"Okay, thanks." Scott gave her the address.

"I'll look forward to meeting her." Sarah quickly ran a mental checklist of the errands she'd now committed to and decided to go to the Picketts' house first. She grabbed her purse and headed out.

Ten minutes later, she pulled into the driveway of a small ranch house in a fairly new residential neighborhood. The lot was quite large, and snow-covered bushes lined the walk. Not a bad starter house for a young couple.

Soon after Sarah knocked, a dark-haired young woman in jeans and a green sweater opened the front door. The little boy she held on her hip quickly buried his face in the woman's shoulder.

"You must be McKenna," Sarah said.

The young woman smiled, and Sarah was struck by how pretty she was. "That's right. And you're Sarah Hart."

"Yes."

"Won't you come in?" McKenna stepped back, gently patting the little boy's back.

Sarah followed them inside and closed the door, shutting out the January chill. As McKenna turned to lead Sarah down the hall, the little boy's eyes peeked over his mother's shoulder.

"Hello there." Sarah waved at the toddler.

He hid his face again, but Sarah heard a little giggle. His hair was lighter than McKenna's, and he had the warm brown eyes Sarah was beginning to recognize as a family trait.

"I'm pleased to meet you," Sarah said.

"Come on, Caleb." McKenna disentangled his arms from around her neck and turned so she faced Sarah. "He's a little shy. I've got the flannel shirts right here." She picked up a plastic store bag from the sofa and adjusted Caleb's weight so that he sat on her other hip.

Sarah reached for the bag. "Thank you."

"Oh, it's I who should be thanking you. It's very nice of you to make a quilt for Grandpa Vern."

"I'll have fun doing it."

"Well, I put in three shirts. Scott said it was all right to give you ones that were showing wear."

"Certainly." She glanced around. The living room furnishings were inexpensive—probably some hand-me-downs and garage sale finds among them—but vibrant curtains and cushions brightened the room, and several baskets held magazines and potted houseplants. A couple of framed photos sat on top of a bookcase. One was a studio portrait of Caleb, and the other was a black-and-white snapshot of two men. "I love your basket collection."

"Thank you. Would you like to sit down for a minute?" McKenna flashed her smile again.

"I really should go on and get my errands done. Is that a picture of Vern?"

"Yes." McKenna picked it up and took it to Sarah. "That's him and one of his army pals, I guess."

Sarah studied it. The two men in olive drab uniforms looked almost too young to be in military service. She could easily tell which one was Vern. "Those eyes are distinctive. He must have been a charmer back then."

McKenna laughed. "Yeah, like Scott." Sarah handed her the frame, and she set it down. "I hope the shirts work out okay. One of them is torn."

"Let me just take a quick peek." Sarah opened the bag and drew out the shirts. The torn one was mostly red and black, one was predominantly green, and the third was a red and blue mix. "These will work just fine, and I'll fill in the rest of the squares with scraps I have or remnants of new material."

"Are you sure?" McKenna asked. "The one looks pretty frayed on the collar and cuffs."

"That's all right. I'll use the parts that are still strong. They may be past their prime for wearing, but there's still a lot of life in them."

"Scott was really taken with the quilt he saw at the nursing home," McKenna said. "He doesn't usually get excited about things like that, but I think he saw how much it could mean to his grandfather."

"Scott seems like a thoughtful young man," Sarah said.

"He is, and he's been very concerned about making Grandpa feel comfortable at Bradford Manor."

"I hope the quilt will be a comfort to him—a remembrance, as well as a warm blanket." Sarah paused. "McKenna, I don't want to be nosy, but may I ask you something about Grandpa Vern?"

"Sure."

"I saw the picture he carries around—the woman named Alice Ward."

McKenna nodded. "I've seen it."

"I don't know what Alice means to him," Sarah said, "but he seemed to regret deeply that he never found her after the war. I'm curious about that."

McKenna shrugged. "What can I say? Scott and I never heard of her until...oh, maybe a year or so ago. Then all of a sudden he started talking about her. How he should have gone and found her, that sort of thing."

"How badly do you think he wants to find her?" Sarah hesitated. "Because sometimes I help people with things like that. But I didn't press Vern about it, and Scott seemed uncomfortable when I mentioned Alice."

McKenna sighed and set Caleb on the rug. The little boy bent over and began tugging at the Velcro closing on the side of his shoe.

"I thought at first it might help Grandpa if we could find her, so I tried searching online for him, but it seems the Ward family doesn't live in Concord anymore."

"Concord?" Sarah stopped replacing the shirts in the bag. "I guess I assumed she was from around here."

"Grandpa Vern grew up in Concord. That's where he knew Alice. But when I told him I didn't find anything about her family there, he seemed a little agitated, and it seemed better to just stop talking about it, so I haven't brought it up again. I really didn't have time to do any more on it, anyway, but—" She eyed Sarah. "You said you help find people?"

"No, that's not what I meant exactly. I've helped a few people, solved a few little mysteries." Sarah waved a hand, not wanting to give her penchant for sleuthing more credit than was due.

"You're like a detective?" McKenna's eyes went round.

"No, not really." Sarah chuckled. "I'm persistent is all. If someone like Vern wanted some help with a—well, you could call it a mystery, I suppose—I could do a little investigating and see if I could turn up any information. It's a hobby of mine. But I don't like to poke into people's business if they don't want me to."

"That's interesting." Caleb had pulled his shoe off, and McKenna stooped and slipped it back on.

"I'd better get going," Sarah said.

McKenna looked up at her. "Do you mind if I tell Scott what you said? I mean, if it would help Grandpa feel better to know what became of this Alice person, maybe it would be worth doing."

"Sure. But I don't want to upset either Vern or Scott. I'll be sewing the quilt, and I won't mention Alice to Vern again if Scott thinks it's a bad idea."

McKenna straightened. "Thanks. We'll be in touch."

Sarah backed out of the driveway, eager now to get to the next destination. Now that she'd seen Vern's shirts, she could look for complementary fabrics at Wild Goose Chase or even try to hunt for some extra flannel shirts at the thrift store. But first she'd stop by the church to pick up Angela's Sunday school materials.

She drove to Bridge Street and rolled past the pastor's house to the church.

She eased her car into the parking lot near the side door of the church. That entrance was nearest the pastor's study. The pavement had been plowed after the last storm, but the surface glittered. The sun must have melted some of the

snow in the last few days, and then it refroze as treacherous ice, as smooth as a polished tabletop. Sarah let the snow
tires on her Pontiac feel for traction as the car inched forward. She glanced ahead toward where she wanted to end
up and caught her breath.

On the ground near the side door lay the dark, still form
of a man in a winter overcoat.

CHAPTER THREE

S arah jammed on the brakes and instantly regretted it. Her car slewed sideways a couple of feet. She took her foot off the brake and let the Grand Prix ease to a stop, then put the transmission in PARK. She grabbed her cell phone and got out of the car.

Hurrying toward the unmoving figure, she nearly lost her balance and dropped her phone on the slippery pavement. She pulled up short and eyed the ground for a less treacherous path across the ice, stooped to retrieve her phone, and inched her way toward him.

When she got close, her fears were realized. The man lying on the icy pavement was Pastor John. She knelt beside him and shook his shoulder gently.

"John? Are you hurt?"

His hat was askew, partly hiding his face. She lifted it. His face held a pallor that made her heart skip a beat.

"John?" She lifted his left hand, put her fingers to his wrist, and sat, not breathing, for several seconds, until she felt his pulse. Almost immediately she saw his chest rise as he drew in a breath. "Thank you, Lord." She opened her phone and dialed 911.

She glanced about as it rang and noted a plastic bucket with a fireplace shovel sticking out of it. The pastor must have been throwing sand on the icy parking lot.

She looked down at him again. His face was still drawn, and his eyes remained shut.

"Nine-one-one, what is your emergency?"

"I have a man who's fallen on the ice and is unconscious. Could you please send an ambulance to Bridge Street Church? Thank you."

"Ma'am, do you know how long he's been unconscious?" the operator asked.

"No, I don't know how long he's been lying on the ground." Still holding the phone to her ear and answering the dispatcher's questions, Sarah got to her feet and baby-stepped to the sand bucket. She took a shovelful of sand and sprinkled it before her as she walked slowly toward her car. She took her plaid wool throw from the backseat and carried it back to the pastor, wondering if she could somehow get him onto it.

He moaned and blinked as she reached him. She knelt beside him and flipped the blanket over his legs and torso. Pain radiated from his green eyes. "Sarah. What happened?"

"He's conscious," Sarah said into the phone. She bent toward Pastor John. "I'm glad to see you awake. I've called an ambulance. What hurts?"

He hesitated and tried to raise his head, but he winced and lowered it again. "My ankle, at least. It hurts a lot."

An approaching siren wailed. Sarah told the dispatcher that John was lucid and what he had said. With help close by, she wouldn't try to get him onto the blanket, but would wait and let the experts do the moving. She signed off and put her phone in her pocket as the ambulance pulled slowly into the lot. She waved to the driver. The vehicle rolled slowly closer to where Pastor John lay.

"Watch the glare ice," Sarah called as a female EMT opened the passenger door.

The two technicians carefully crossed the pavement. They spoke to the pastor and took his vital signs. Sarah sprinkled some more sand between where they worked and the vehicles. After what seemed entirely too long, they prepared to load the pastor onto their stretcher and into the ambulance.

"Is there someone you'd like contacted, sir?" the EMT asked.

Pastor John looked around and focused on Sarah. "Perhaps one of the deacons?"

"Of course. I'll ask them to go to the hospital. Is there anything else you need done immediately?"

"I can't think of anything. Oh! Angela's Sunday school material. It's on my desk." He grimaced as the EMTs rolled him toward the back of the ambulance.

Sarah smiled at his efficiency, even in a time of crisis. "I'll get it. Don't you worry about a thing."

At quarter past one, Sarah lingered at the table with her friend Martha Maplethorpe. After calling a few key people in the church, she'd gone to Martha's for consolation and wound up staying for lunch with Martha and her husband Ernie.

Sarah's cell phone rang, and she fished it out of her purse. Head deacon Harry Butler's name showed on the screen.

"The pastor needs surgery on that ankle," Harry said. "It's broken, and they need to set the bone. His wrist is sprained, too, and they've got that wrapped, but I don't think Pastor John is going anywhere for a while. He's got quite a bump on his head, so they're going to watch him pretty closely for a couple of days."

A few moments later, Sarah relayed Harry's news to Martha and Ernie. "He said it would be good if someone could set up a schedule of people to take meals to the pastor after he goes home from the hospital."

"I can do that." Martha's eyes shone with eagerness. "I'll start calling the ladies right now. Will he be home this weekend?"

"Harry wasn't sure. But the way it sounded, Pastor John may not go home until Monday. The nurse told him it will depend on how the surgery goes."

Martha was already reaching for a tablet and a pen. She'd do a good job, Sarah knew—Martha had organized the Holiday Home Tour this past year, and she'd done a fantastic job. She'd had a couple of weeks to recuperate since the Christmas rush, and now she seized the new project with an energy Sarah didn't feel.

"Is the pastor up to having visitors?" Ernie asked. "I'd be happy to stop by and spend some time with Pastor John."

"A couple of the other men are at the hospital with Harry now. He said the doctors plan to do the surgery in the morning."

Martha didn't look up from the notes she was jotting on her pad. "If anyone asks, I'll tell them to hold off on visiting at least until late tomorrow. Could you let the prayer chain leaders know?" Martha asked.

Sarah nodded. "Certainly. I have the list at home. Oh, and Harry also said he's got one of the other fellows working on lining up a speaker for Sunday morning." Sarah looked at her watch. "Look at the time! I was going to go buy some fabric today. I'd better get moving."

The bell on the door of Wild Goose Chase rang cheerfully as Sarah entered the store. The riot of color always excited her.

Fabrics, yarns, thread, and notions of all sorts beckoned to her.

"Hello!" Vanessa laid down the paperback she'd been reading and hurried from behind the counter. "It's been slow today. Glad to see a real, live customer."

"Well, I'm primed to buy." Sarah squinted at the book and tried to read the title upside down. "What are you reading?"

Vanessa smiled. "*The Crusader's Castle.*" She picked up the book and turned it so that Sarah could see the cover. A pale, blonde maiden stood on the rampart of a castle tower, looking out over a rugged landscape. "Remember that book I lent you a couple of weeks ago? Same author."

Vanessa had recently been pushing Sarah to read a few of her favorite authors. Sarah had finally caved when Vanessa showed her the cover of the author's first book, which was free of ramparts and medieval landscapes.

"Oh, that's right," Sarah said. "I haven't gotten to it yet, but I will."

Vanessa shrugged. "No rush. If we get snowed in this weekend like the weatherman is saying, you'll have plenty of time."

"Right," Sarah said. Her personal taste fell more toward mysteries than the historical novels Vanessa liked so much, but she'd give this one a try. "I'm starting a new quilt similar to the one I made my dad, and I need some more material."

"Oh, you finished the birthday quilt?"

"Yes. I just delivered it to Dad at Bradford Manor yesterday. He seemed pleased."

"What did you use for backing on that?"

"A flannel sheet. I should have brought it in to show you, but I took pictures. I cut up four of his old flannel shirts. They were getting thin on the elbows, but the fronts and back were still good. And I left the pockets on, and a few buttons, for a nostalgic, country look."

"I'll bet it's really cute," Vanessa said.

Sarah nodded. "In a masculine sort of way, yes."

"I think it was a lovely idea."

"Thank you." Sarah chose four flannel plaids and a spool of quilting thread, then made a quick foray through Vanessa's remnant bin. She took her finds to the counter.

Vanessa measured out half a yard from each bolt of flannel and rang up Sarah's purchases. "Stay warm."

Sarah laughed. "Thanks. You too!"

"Thanks for stopping by," Vanessa said.

Sarah checked the time and decided to put off visiting the thrift shop. That might be something Amy and Audrey, her twin granddaughters, would enjoy doing with her one of these days. Instead she turned the car toward home.

About six o'clock, snug in her Queen Anne house on Hillside Avenue, she sat down to supper with Belle. The young woman worked long hours at the Copy Shop in town, but she and Sarah spent an evening or two a week together. The pastor's predicament dampened their mood somewhat. Belle attended Bridge Street Church with Sarah when her schedule allowed, and she'd found the news of Pastor John's accident distressing.

"I'm so glad you went to the church when you did," she told Sarah.

"Yes. If I'd gone earlier, I wouldn't have been there to help him after he fell. And if I'd waited until after I did the shopping..."

"No kidding. Would you tell Martha to put me down for some cookies? I'm not around at the right times to take a meal over, but I could make cookies and have them ready in the freezer anytime."

"I'm sure both Martha and Pastor John would appreciate that."

When they'd cleaned up the kitchen, Sarah settled before the fireplace with the Sunday school manual while Belle took out a puzzle book.

Sarah studied the lesson and appropriate scripture passage for about an hour, then put her materials aside. Angela had prepared visuals for the lesson and left a folder of activity sheets and take-home papers for the children, and Sarah felt she'd be well prepared if she put in one more study session before Sunday.

"I think I'll do a little work in my sewing room." She stretched her arms and arched her back. "I get too lazy if I sit by the fire for long."

Belle chuckled. "I know what you mean. But it's such a perfect January evening."

"I'm going to make some tea. Would you like a cup?"

"I'd love it. Thank you."

Sarah went to the warm cranberry-and-cream kitchen and put the teakettle on the stove. She walked into her sewing room and woke her computer from its sleep mode while the water heated.

Once she had delivered Belle's cup of tea, she carried her own back into the sewing room and picked up the bag McKenna Pickett had given her. She pulled out the three shirts and examined them visually, then tugged gently on the fabric to judge its strength. She didn't want to put any pieces in the quilt that were going to fall apart the first time it was washed.

Satisfied with the shirts, she laid out the black and red one on her cutting table and smoothed the fabric. She could make several squares from the front and back, and she wanted to include one of the pockets, and perhaps part of a cuff as well. This one hadn't begun to fray.

As she ran her hand over the front, something crackled beneath her hand.

"Well, Vern, what did you leave in your pocket?"

She unbuttoned the flap and carefully extracted a folded sheet of paper. It probably wasn't anything important—after all, it must have been there since before Vern's fall several weeks ago. Still, it might be something he had meant to deal with and forgot.

She unfolded the paper and smoothed it out on top of the shirt. It appeared to be a computer-printed invitation. "Report for Duty and Fun," read the large letters at the top, with a small picture of a GI in combat uniform below it.

Sarah reached for her reading glasses and focused on the smaller print beneath the picture. "Attention, all personnel of the 182nd Massachusetts. Our annual reunion will be held this year in Worcester. Don't miss it!" The flyer continued with a list of planned activities and a form to submit for a dinner reservation. The reunion wasn't for a couple of months yet.

Was Vern planning to attend his unit's reunion? He obviously had not sent in his reservation. Sarah frowned over the paper and read it again. The deadline for signing up for the dinner was February 1. She considered taking the paper to Vern, but then he would wonder where she'd gotten it. Scott seemed to want to keep the quilt a surprise, so she couldn't tell Vern about McKenna giving her a bag of his shirts.

Finally she decided the best thing to do would be to call Scott's house and tell him what she had found. If he thought Vern hoped to attend the reunion or simply wanted the invitation for the contact information it contained, she could deliver it to him or McKenna.

It wasn't quite eight o'clock, so she placed the call to the Pickett house. Scott answered, and Sarah quickly explained about the invitation to the army unit's reunion.

"Oh, you can probably just toss that," he said. "Grandpa told me he didn't want to go."

"Really? He seems so fond of his time in the service. Doesn't he want to see his old buddies?"

"As far as I know, he's never been to one of those things."

Odd that he had saved the invitation if he didn't care about the event. "Well, if you're sure ... "

"I'm pretty certain. He got it quite a while ago—before Thanksgiving, I think. He must have stuck it in that pocket and forgotten about it. He's never kept in touch with anyone from his regiment."

"You think he'd enjoy seeing some of them?"

"I said something to that effect, and he said most of the men he knew are gone now."

"I suppose that's true. Sixty-six years since the end of the war."

"Yeah, I think it's safe to throw it away."

Sarah hesitated. Vern hadn't seen Alice Ward for at least that long, and he still cared about her. She laid the paper on her computer desk and decided to broach the topic that had kept buzzing around her mind all day, between the pastor's accident, the Sunday school lesson, and her errands.

"Scott, did McKenna mention to you the conversation we had this morning?"

"Well, yeah, she did."

Sarah waited, but he didn't say any more. "If you don't want to talk about it, that's okay. And I promise I won't mention it again."

"You mean Alice," he said a bit warily.

"Yes. She seems to be on his mind a lot."

"Well ... yes, I suppose so."

"Would it hurt if I did a little sleuthing? If we could find out what happened to her, it might ease his mind."

Scott sighed. "I wish he'd just forget about her. But you're right—he's been talking about her for a while now, and he keeps looking at that picture. After you left the home yesterday, he brought her up again. The woman is probably dead by now, but I guess it's possible that she's not."

"If he knew she was dead, he'd stop wondering," Sarah said. "And if we discovered she was alive…"

"We?"

Sarah took a breath. "Well, I thought I might be able to do some searching for her online or at the library—just simple things I've learned to help locate people. But I'd need more information from you or Vern."

Another long pause followed. Sarah was afraid he had hung up, or the connection was lost.

"Scott? I'm only asking because I think your grandpa's lonely. He misses your grandmother, I'm sure, and he may be wishing for someone he cared about—an old friend—you know, someone he has shared memories with."

Sarah knew the loneliness that came when a spouse died. The first year after Gerry died had been the worst, when she would sometimes wake up in the middle of the night and hold his pillow while she cried. She still missed him horribly, but friends and family members filled some of the void for her. At least Vern had Scott and his family nearby. Sarah's son Jason and his family had recently moved to Maple Hill, and their nearness comforted her. But a friend your own age was special. She hoped Scott would give her his blessing to hunt for answers for the lonely old man.

At last he said, "I suppose it wouldn't hurt to do a little looking. But I don't want him to get all worked up about it."

"Why don't you tell me everything you know about Alice, and I'll see if I can find any clues without even mentioning it to Vern."

"I don't know much."

Sarah pushed gently. "Your grandfather knew her when he was a child, is that right?"

"A child? I don't know about that, but I'm pretty sure they went to high school together. She was his girlfriend then, or at least he liked her at lot."

"And McKenna told me that Vern grew up in Concord. Is that right?"

"Yeah. That's what he told me." He paused, and Sarah was about to speak when he added, "The only thing I really know is she had a car."

"A car? That was unusual for a girl in those days."

"Yeah, but Grandpa's mentioned it more than once. A blue Chevy."

A girl in the thirties with a blue Chevy. What was she getting herself into?

"I'll do a little sleuthing. And I'll let you know if I find anything before telling Vern, okay?"

"I guess so."

"Will you call me if you think of anything else?"

"Sure. Oh, hey, there is something. There was a kid named Bob that he hung around with too. I don't know his last name, but they were good friends. Grandpa told me they would go swimming together in the summer."

Sarah scribbled on her pad, glad Scott was opening up, and trying to picture a very young Vern—the young man in the photo McKenna had shown her—behind the wheel of his girlfriend's Chevy. Being noticed by a pretty girl who had her own car must have been heady stuff for the young man. She recalled the thrill she'd felt when Gerry had begun to notice her. A story lay behind Vern's relationship with Alice, she was certain. But would investigating it upset people?

She hoped not. Stirring up bad feelings was the last thing she wanted to do. But the possibility of reuniting two people who'd loved each other so long ago intrigued her. Her grandfather had been separated from her grandmother for many years, and only recently Sarah had learned what had become of her grandmother Molly Drayton. No one should have to go through the pain her grandfather had known—losing a loved one and never knowing why.

An Internet search for Alice Ward in Concord turned up nothing that looked promising—McKenna had been right about that. The white pages listed four Wards in Concord. She wrote down the numbers in her notepad.

The next morning, Sarah decided to take her quest elsewhere. A trip to the public library had often helped with her mysteries. Maybe it would help her now. Eagerly she put her scanty notes in a folder and put on her parka and gloves.

A few minutes later, she pulled up in front of the stone library building. Before getting out of the car, she called Martha.

"Hi! Any news on the pastor this morning?"

"I talked to Harry Butler's wife Elaine," Martha said. "Harry called the nurses' station this morning, and they told him Pastor John's surgery was on schedule."

"Great. I'm going into the library now, but would you have time to meet for coffee later?"

"Sounds good," Martha said. "Liam's at ten?"

"Perfect." Sarah hurried inside the two-story building. The smells of old books, ink, and furniture polish greeted her. Sarah loved the old library with its high ceilings and cozy seats for reading in corners between the tall bookshelves.

"Sarah!" Spencer Hewitt grinned at her from behind the circulation desk. "When you come in, it's always an adventure. How can I help you today?"

Sarah squeezed her lips together for a moment. "I'm looking for some old friends of an elderly man who grew up in Concord. I don't know much about them. One was a girl named Alice Ward. She's not listed in the directory, which isn't surprising. Any ideas?"

"Hmm." Spencer leaned on the other side of the desk. "How old is this person?"

"She'd be in her eighties now, but she probably got married and changed her last name years ago." She pointed to her notes. "I'm considering going down the list of Wards in the phone book and making cold calls to inquire about Alice. But you know, I hate to bother people, and I wouldn't want to disturb anyone if she was one of their loved ones and she'd recently passed away."

Spencer nodded. "Anything else?"

"There was also a boy named Bob. I don't know his last name, but he was probably in the same school as Alice and my friend Vern."

"What about annuals?"

Sarah blinked at him. Her first thought was the flowering plants she bought each spring—impatiens, snapdragons, petunias. That couldn't be what Spencer meant. "Oh. Yearbooks." She laughed. "Of course. I could look for Alice Ward and her friend Vern in yearbooks."

"That's what I was thinking. And you could probably glean a little more information about them if you found them. Maybe enough to make some of those calls to the right people. Maybe younger siblings of theirs who still live in town."

"Great idea. You wouldn't happen to have Concord yearbooks, would you?"

Spencer shook his head. "No. But I know someone who can help you."

"Who's that?"

"Laura Baird at the Concord Free Public Library. She's their research librarian."

"Wow. They're big enough to have a special librarian just for research?" Sarah asked.

"Oh, yes. A lot of people go to Concord to research the famous writers who lived there. Emerson, Thoreau, Louisa May Alcott..."

"Of course. Maybe I could make a trip over there soon." Sarah didn't relish the long drive, but was willing to put in the time to help Vern.

"That would be great, and I know you love digging into things yourself. But it would be easier, faster, and less expensive to make a well-directed call."

"You're right."

Spencer smiled and nodded toward her notebook. "So. Want to write the names down for me, and the years they would have been in high school? I'll call Laura and ask if she can help us."

While Spencer looked up the number and dialed, Sarah wrote the names Vern Pickett, Bob ?, and Alice Ward on a fresh slip of paper and thought about when they would have been in high school. Without more information, she'd need to inquire about a range of several years.

Spencer hung up a minute later with a frown. "I'm sorry. She's not working this morning. The head librarian said he'll leave a note for Laura to call you. I left your home phone number."

Sarah gathered her notes and closed the folder. "Thank you, Spencer." She smiled at him. "Maybe I should just go over there. I could drive to Concord in three hours."

"True. But if Laura finds some solid leads for you, you could think about driving over next week to interview people who knew these folks you're looking for."

Sarah thought about Alice and Vern. "You know, I'm not sure what year they would have graduated, or even if they were in the same class. Vern served in the war, but I don't know how old he was when he enlisted. Maybe I'd better talk to him again."

"Why don't you figure it out as best you can? When Laura calls you, you can ask her for the years you think are most likely."

"That's good advice. Thanks."

Sarah went to the stacks and browsed the section on World War II, focusing on the books that covered the Pacific campaign. At last she checked out a book that included the fighting at Guadalcanal, said good-bye to Spencer, and headed for her car. If only it weren't so far to Concord. But with a big snowstorm coming, she couldn't consider a trip like that anyway. Maybe Spencer was right. Next week. After the roads were clear and the skies were sunny again.

A few minutes later, she entered The Spotted Dog and stooped to pat Murphy, the resident Corgi, in the bookstore side of the business. When she straightened, she looked around for Martha.

Liam Connolly, the owner of the café and bookstore, came over smiling broadly. "Sarah, my dear, 'tis a pleasure to see you on this chilly morning."

"Thank you, Liam. It's great to see you too. Is Martha here?"

"Haven't seen her."

Sarah glanced at her watch. "Well, I'm expecting her, but I'm about ten minutes early."

"Ah. Can I get you something while you wait?" Liam walked Sarah over to an empty table.

Sarah let him seat her. "A chai latte for me, please."

"A good choice." Liam winked at her. "I'll keep my eyes peeled for sweet Martha."

Sarah laughed as he walked away and pulled out the book she'd chosen at the library. She skimmed the first chapter, then turned to the section on Guadalcanal, an island in the Solomon Islands chain and the scene of fierce fighting from August 1942 to February 1943.

"Am I late?" Martha set her purse and crocheting bag on an empty chair and took off her coat.

"Not at all." Sarah closed the book. Maybe she'd have time to read more later.

Karen Bancroft, a part-time waitress at the café, came over, and Martha gave her order.

"How's the meal schedule for Pastor John coming?" Sarah asked.

Martha shrugged. "It's a little tougher to get volunteers than I anticipated, but we'll make it."

"Well, put me down in the first slot you haven't filled."

"Really? Thanks. How about tomorrow?"

Sarah eyed her in surprise. "That soon? Sure, it's no problem."

Martha exhaled deeply. "Thank you. I've got people on tap for Monday and Tuesday, but I just found out he's coming home tomorrow after all, and no one seemed flexible enough to cook for him Saturday."

"Wow. That seems awfully soon after surgery."

Martha pulled out the schedule of meals she had lined up so far, and Sarah suggested a few other church members who might be willing to help.

"I'm going to set up a chart on my computer for this," Martha said. "Do you think there's anything else that needs to be done for Sunday that we haven't thought of?"

"I don't know." Sarah frowned, trying to read the list upside down. "You might want to check with Harry and see if we need someone to host the guest speaker for dinner after."

"Good thinking." Martha looked up as Liam came toward them carrying a tray with their steaming drinks on it. "Hello, Liam. Where'd Karen go?" Martha asked, looking toward the counter.

"She had to leave to get to class in time. Besides, I wanted an excuse to serve two lovely ladies."

"Oh, listen to you." Martha waved a hand at him as he set their mugs on the table.

Sarah was about to make a cheerful retort when her cell phone rang. "Oh, excuse me." She took it out and glanced at the screen, but didn't recognize the local number. "Hello?"

"Sarah Hart?"

"Yes." She tried to place the gruff masculine voice.

"This is Vern Pickett. We need to talk."

CHAPTER FOUR

The unexpected drive to Bradford Manor gave Sarah time to think of several reasons why Vern had summoned her. Most likely was that he was angry with her. She had finished her tea with Martha but left shortly after. She hoped she hadn't cut short the time she might have spent with her friend just to be yelled at.

Snow lay on top of Bradford Manor's roof like a blanket and muffled the sound of her footsteps up the front walk. Vern surprised her when she entered the lobby. He was sitting near the aviary in his wheelchair, watching the door like a cat ready to pounce on whatever peeped out of a mouse hole.

"There you are."

She pulled up short as he pushed his chair toward her. "Hello, Vern." She looked around, hoping they wouldn't disturb the half dozen residents sitting in the lounge area. "What's this about?"

He pointed an accusing finger at her, his gray eyebrows pulling together. "You've been talking about me."

She pursed her lips. "Yes, I have. I'm sorry if that upset you."

He let out his breath, deflating and slumping in his chair. "I'm not upset. Not now. I was at first, but ..."

"May I take you over to the sitting area?" Sarah asked.

"Thanks."

She pushed him along without speaking. When they reached a casual grouping of chairs, Sarah turned the wheelchair and sat down in the extra chair beside him.

"Believe me, Vern, it wasn't my intention to sneak around behind your back or to do anything underhanded."

"Scotty said he wasn't going to tell me, but he was afraid I'd be mad when I found out. He said if I didn't want you to go ahead with this, I could call you and tell you to stop."

"Is that why you called me?"

He sighed, looking toward the window. "When Scotty told me, I was riled. But ... well, if you really think you can find something useful."

"I can't guarantee anything, but I'm willing to try. But only if you want me to."

He nodded and met her gaze for a moment before he spoke. "I guess it's time to admit I can't do it alone and accept some help."

"Do you really want to find her, Vern? Or is it just a distraction from all of this?" Sarah waved her arm, indicating Bradford Manor, his health issues, and his solitude.

He seemed to understand. "Yes. I want to know what happened to her." His voice caught, and Sarah felt a lump form in her throat. She laid a hand on his arm.

"You realize she may have passed away a long time ago."

Vern nodded and slid two fingers into the pocket of his green plaid shirt. He extracted the picture of Alice and looked down at it before offering it to Sarah. "Do you think you could find out anything about her even if she's already gone?"

She took the picture and studied the young woman's face. Such expressive eyes. Softly waved dark hair floated about her shoulders, but was rolled back off her forehead. Sarah flipped the photo over. "Love, Alice" was written in faded pencil. She turned it over again. "How old was she when this was taken?"

"Seventeen."

Sarah's heart contracted at the emotion in his voice, though Vern was still mostly a stranger to her. She was drawn to puzzles without much bait, and a romantic puzzle was irresistible. She couldn't walk away from Vern's situation. If there was any possible way to reunite him with Alice, or at least to put his mind at ease concerning Alice's fate, she would do it.

She considered the photo for another moment. The girl had been pretty, and no doubt popular. Sarah could tell the picture had seen a lot of wear. One corner was creased, and the picture curled slightly. The girl's hairstyle and dress collar took her back—way back. Alice looked well groomed and right in fashion for her time.

"I could probably find out something, though I couldn't promise. You'd have to tell me more, of course."

"What do you need to know?"

"Let me get something to write on." She opened her purse and took out a small notebook and a pen. "Tell me about her."

"Well…" Vern looked off toward the window again. Frost glittered on the outside of the panes. Outside Bradford Manor, the sun sparkled on crusty snow. The gardens were hidden beneath the cottony layer, but the grounds still gave them a charming view of Maple Hill below them and mountains in the distance. "We went to school together."

"Yes." She smiled and made a note. "What else can you tell me? Do you know when she was born?"

He frowned. "Can't say I do. Not the exact day. I probably knew it back then." He shook his head. "But she was seventeen in nineteen forty-one. I know that. That, and she had a nineteen thirty-nine Chevy. Blue."

His dreamy smile told Sarah volumes about Vern's feelings for Alice, and she didn't think it was just because of the car.

"Okay, that's a start. What about her family?"

"Hmm…"

Vern was quiet for a long time. "My memory isn't what it used to be. I...don't recall much. Her folks were wealthy."

"Did she have brothers or sisters?"

He sighed. "Can't remember. Sorry." His eyes brightened and he raised his chin. "She had a friend, though. Her best friend was named Joan."

"That's a help. Do you remember Joan's last name?"

"Afraid not. Alice would pick her up and they'd drive to school together."

"I guess you realize Alice probably married someone."

"Yeah, I've thought about that. She'd have a different name now. I guess that would make it hard to find her."

"Harder, but not impossible. Can you tell me anything else about her friend Joan?"

"Hmm. Not really."

"Scott said you had a friend named Bob."

His eyes flickered. "Right. Bob Willis. Haven't seen him since 1941. But we used to do everything together. Played ball, rode bikes, that kind of stuff."

"Have you had any contact with Bob since the end of the war?"

"No." Vern looked away again, with no explanation. Maybe Bob didn't make it through the war.

"I'll see if I can find Bob, too, then. He might know something about Alice." Sarah watched his face. Vern made no objection, so she wrote it down. Bob, at least, wouldn't have changed his last name the way Alice probably had. She found it odd that Vern hadn't looked up his old buddy, if he had such fond memories.

"Why didn't you go back to live in Concord, Vern?"

He shook his head. "My mother died, my sister moved away ... by the time I was able, it just didn't seem right."

"But Alice ... the two of you had been close before you went away, hadn't you?"

"Well, we liked each other a lot. We weren't exactly going steady—I couldn't afford a class ring. But I wasn't looking at any other girls, and I'm pretty sure she wasn't seeing anyone else, either. At first I thought she was out of my league, but ..." He paused for a moment, then nodded. "She liked me a lot. Her letters ..."

"You wrote to her after you enlisted?"

"Yeah. We made some plans."

"To get married?"

"Well, I didn't actually propose or anything. I was going to do that when I got back. But she, uh ... she said she was waiting for me."

Sarah tucked that away to think about later. "What went wrong?"

He exhaled deeply. "Things were bad in the Pacific. Worse conditions than I'd ever imagined. I just ..." He let it trail off and stared toward the window.

Sarah waited, but he didn't resume his explanation. Gently, she said, "I've been doing a little reading about the war in the Pacific. You said you served at Guadalcanal. Was that in nineteen forty-two?"

His expression darkened and his lips thinned. "Yeah. Forty-two and forty-three. My regiment was late getting there. After Pearl Harbor, the Navy didn't have enough ships to transport the troops. We went to New Caledonia first. My unit was there quite awhile. Eventually they got us over to Guadalcanal to help the First Marines." He shook his head. "The Marines did a lot of the dirty work, but the Japanese were trying to build airfields on the island. They wanted a big air base there, so they could strike ships going to Australia and New Zealand, I guess. Keep those countries from sending ships out too." He shrugged. "We still met a lot of resistance after we got there."

"It must have been a terrible time. I'm glad you came through it all right."

He nodded. "Thanks. I was wounded, but..."

"I didn't know that. I'm sorry." She looked at him with a new empathy.

"Well, I'm here. There's a lot who aren't."

Perhaps his wound had something to do with the reason he'd ended the relationship with Alice. She decided to change the subject and talk about more pleasant memories. "You said you went to Concord High School?"

"Uh...yes. That's correct."

Sarah frowned. He sounded almost unsure. "And did you graduate the same year as Alice Ward?"

"Well, I..." His gaze wandered to the TV for a moment. "That is..."

Sarah asked gently, "What year was your class, Vern?"

"Hmm. Well, I . . . Alice was seventeen in 1941."

"Yes, you told me that."

He bit his upper lip. After a moment, his face cleared. "She was in my chemistry class, so yes, same class." He smiled as though pleased with himself for remembering. "We were lab partners once or twice."

Sarah smiled. "So . . . did the two of you graduate in 1941?"

"I don't think so. Forty-two. That would be it. I think."

Sarah leaned closer. "So your class was the class of '42. And Bob and Joan were seniors that year too?"

"No. No, that's not right." Vern scratched his head. "It would have been . . . hmm . . . well, maybe you're right. Alice would have graduated . . ." He grimaced and shot her an apologetic glance. "I'm sorry. My memory is so fuzzy these days."

Sarah patted his shoulder. "It's all right. Everybody has days like that."

He looked relieved.

"Can you tell me anything else about your classmates, or about Alice in particular?"

"Uh . . . her father was a lawyer. Did I tell you that?"

"No, I don't believe you did." Sarah wrote it in her notebook. An attorney ought to be fairly easy to trace. "Can you recall his name?"

"No." Vern stroked his chin. "She had that car."

"The Chevy," Sarah said.

"Yes. 1939. I'm sure about that."

"And was it new when she got it?"

"Hmm. Let's see now."

Sarah waited. "I'm sure her father bought it used."

Vern eyed her. "Why do you say that?"

"If she was seventeen in 1941, and the car was a 1939 model, then Alice would have been fifteen or even fourteen when the car was new."

"True, true. They do build cars the year before the model year." Vern paused. "I'm not much help today, am I?"

"Well, learning about her father being an attorney might help me. I should be able to look him up. Do you remember any other classmates?"

"I told you about Bob Willis."

"Yes, you did. And you said he was in your class and Alice's."

Vern's face squeezed up. "I think so. Yes, we did a lot of things together. And he was in our science lab too."

"Do you remember the chemistry teacher's name?"

"Chemistry? No, can't say as I do. Sorry. Do you need to know that?"

"No, not really. I just thought it would help me pinpoint the time if I knew what teachers you had." Sarah nodded and stood. "All right. I'll tell you what, Vern. If I leave you a notebook and a pen, would you write down anything else you remember about school? Anything at all. Names, classes you took, cars your friends had ... anything."

"I can do that," he said. "I have a notepad."

"All right, thanks. I've put in an inquiry with the research librarian in Concord. I'm hoping she'll help me get some answers for you."

"Oh." Vern swallowed and looked up at her. "All right. Thank you."

Sarah held out the photo of Alice. "Here you go. I'll see what I can find."

He looked at the picture in her hand. "Take it with you if you think it will help."

"All right. I'll take good care of it." Sarah was surprised, but this gesture confirmed the depth of Vern's desire to find Alice. She tucked the photograph inside the little notebook and put it away. She thought she had a good chance of finding Alice Ward, if she was still alive, or at least of learning more about her. She turned toward the door.

"She got all A's her junior year."

"What?" Sarah turned around.

"Alice. She got all A's her junior year. That's why her father bought her the car."

"Good. That's very good. Thank you, Vern. If you think of anything else—"

"I know. Write it down."

She pointed at him and smiled. "You got it."

She left him and walked slowly down the hall. Vern's memory trouble seemed just the opposite of her father's.

On good days, Dad could recall all sorts of details about his school chums and childhood neighbors, yet he couldn't remember what he had for lunch. Vern, on the other hand, seemed to have perfect short-term recall, but barely pulled out his high school best friends' names and wasn't even certain of his own graduation year.

Sarah detoured to her father's room. He sat in his recliner, staring at the television. A cooking show was tuned in.

"Hi, Dad. Are you awake?"

He turned his head. "Hello."

"How are you doing today?" She picked up the remote and muted the sound on the program, then sat down near him, watching his face.

"Ruth?"

"No, I'm Sarah." She reached for his hand. On days like this, when her father mistook her for her mother and seemed disoriented, she thought her heart would break.

Lord, thank you for all the years we've had together. Please meet every need he has now.

She feared these times, when his mind seemed so far away, were preparing her for the final separation.

It won't be forever, Lord. Help me to remember that. We'll see each other again.

She stroked her father's hand. He glanced at her.

"I love you, Dad."

After sitting with him for a few more minutes and talking softly about the family's activities, Sarah got up.

"I'll see you again soon, Dad."

"All right."

She turned the sound up on his television program and left.

That evening, Sarah knew it was time to start making some contacts. Her notebook with the list of phone numbers she'd copied from the Concord telephone book lay next to the computer. She picked it up and frowned over it. She knew she was being impatient waiting for the research librarian to get a start on Vern's mystery. But surely some of these people in Concord would recognize the names of the people she sought.

Lord, I don't know what I can find out about this woman, but I'd like to help Vern. You know what's best for him, so I'll leave it up to you. If you want me to find Alice Ward, then please open some doors for me.

She drew a big breath, picked up the phone and keyed in the number listed as belonging to Matthew Ward. A woman answered on the third ring, and Sarah realized she wasn't ready to explain her mission. Quickly she ordered her thoughts.

"Hello. My name is Sarah Hart, and I'm doing a bit of historical research. I'm looking for information about a Ward family that lived in Concord in the 1940s. Would your family qualify?"

"I don't think so," the woman said. "My husband and I moved here in 1992."

"Oh. So he's not related to Alice Ward, then?"

"Not that I know of."

Sarah's keen disappointment prompted her to seize the notebook from the desk. "Well, I see that there are other people named Ward living there now. The telephone book lists a D. E. Ward and a Lance Ward. Would you know—"

"Lance is our son," the woman said. "He got married a couple of years ago. I don't know about the other one you said."

"Thank you. Oh, and there's a Thomas Ward . . ."

"Don't know him."

"Thank you so much. I'm sorry to bother you." Sarah closed the connection with a sigh and crossed off Matthew and Lance Ward. She took a deep swallow of tea and decided to muster her courage again. She'd try the other two listings for people named Ward. If they didn't pan out, she'd put the puzzle aside for tonight and work on her latest quilting project.

A few minutes later, she closed the notebook in defeat. None of the Wards living in Concord knew anything about Alice and her family. There was Bob Willis, though. She hadn't known his last name before, but she could search for him on the computer now. She opened a search engine and typed in his name and location.

Twelve Robert Willises. Sarah stared at the computer screen for a moment, then printed out the list of Robert Willises residing in Massachusetts. Although none lived in Concord, lots of other Willises did.

The photo of Alice Ward lay with her notes, beside her computer. She gazed at the picture again. What had happened to the lovely young woman? She wished she'd questioned Vern more closely about how they'd lost touch.

Alice smiled up at her from the small photograph that lay on the desk. Sarah picked it up and looked again into the young woman's vibrant eyes. Alice looked confident and ready for whatever life could throw at her.

"I'm going to find you," she said aloud.

The phone rang on the table next to her. She waited a beat, then answered.

"This is Laura Baird in Concord. I had a message from Sarah Hart."

"Yes, this is she. Thank you for calling."

"Spencer Hewitt said you were interested in seeing yearbooks from the old Concord High School. We have them here in the library's reference room, but they can't be lent out."

Sarah frowned. "So, will I have to drive over to Concord?"

"I could look up your students for you and tell you if I find them listed. Now, we also have Concord-Carlisle—that's the new high school in town—and Concord Academy."

"What's that?" Sarah asked. "A private school?"

"Yes. The academy was a school for girls, started in nineteen twenty-two. It's still there, but it went co-ed in nineteen seventy-one. Is it possible that any of the students you're looking for attended the academy instead of the public high school?"

Sarah sank down on a stool at the kitchen island. "I'm pretty sure they all attended the public school. Here are the names I'm searching for: Alice Ward, Bob Willis, and Vern Pickett. And another girl named Joan, last name unknown, who was Alice's best friend. The only date I have is nineteen forty-one—Alice was seventeen that year."

"It's a starting place. This sounds like an interesting search—different from what I usually do. It may be a few days, but I'll call you when I have something."

"That sounds good." Sarah gave Laura her e-mail address. As soon as they'd hung up, she went back to her computer. She did a search for "Ward" and "attorney" in Concord, hoping to find out something about Alice's father, but nothing of any use turned up.

She wasn't sure she was ready to cold-call more strangers tonight. She went out into the living room and sat down with her library book. The descriptions of battles wrenched her stomach. Thinking about boys right out of high school going into those conditions saddened her.

As she turned a page, she found a mention of the Americal Division that Vern had belonged to. While the 1st Marines bore the brunt of the early part of the campaign, they were reinforced by the army's infantry Americal Division in October and November. Sarah jotted a note to look up more about the division when she had time. The Japanese had seized the islands from the British, and the Americans were able to wrest them back. An entire chapter was devoted to the battle tactics and results. Reluctantly, she closed the book.

The backdoor opened and Belle came in. Sarah got up and went to meet her in the kitchen.

"Hi. How was work?"

"Okay. I have tomorrow off, and I thought I'd drive up in the hills and get some pictures."

They chatted a few more minutes, and Belle went upstairs. Sarah went to her sewing room and turned off her computer. She held Alice's picture up for a moment and gave the girl's image a stern look.

"I meant what I said, Alice. I'll find you. Don't think I won't." She tucked the picture into her notebook.

CHAPTER FIVE

"Pastor John's going home from the hospital this morning," Sarah told her son Jason on the phone Saturday morning. "I'm making lunch for him, and I wondered if the girls would like to come over and help."

"That's awfully soon, isn't it?" Jason asked. "I thought they were keeping him at the hospital until Monday."

"I thought so too, but they said he can go home if he has someone to stay with him for a few nights."

"Who's going to do that?"

"Martha got Eddie Davidson. He's still home on college break, and he doesn't have to be back until Tuesday."

"Well, that's good," Jason said.

"Yes. Martha's putting in a lot of work on setting up volunteers. It's turning into rather a large job for her."

The girls were willing to help and Jason said he'd bring them over in an hour, after they'd cleaned up their bedrooms. Sarah tucked her few breakfast dishes into the dishwasher. This might be a good time to work on cutting the squares for Vern's quilt. As she worked, she mulled over everything she'd learned. In the past she'd discovered that not thinking too hard about a problem could help her make connections she hadn't seen at first. Quilting kept her hands busy while her mind wandered and explored. As she worked, cutting and laying the colorful squares side by side to get an impression of how the finished quilt would look, she prayed silently for Pastor John and for her father.

When Jason dropped off the twins, Audrey was animated and full of plans. Amy sat down immediately to browse a cookbook Sarah had left on the island counter. Having her twelve-year-old twin granddaughters around made Sarah feel young and old at the same time. Their energy inspired her but also reminded her that she'd lost some of her old endurance. Even so, she was up to a day of cooking and shopping with these two, no doubt about that.

"Can we make cookies for Pastor John's lunch?" Amy asked.

Audrey rolled her eyes at her sister. "He needs something more than cookies."

"Of course, but for dessert, I mean."

Sarah smiled and opened a cupboard. "I think making cookies is a good idea. We can take him some extras for a snack later on. But for the main course, I was thinking we'd make up a plate with chicken alfredo, green beans, and a biscuit."

"Alfredo? What about that chicken and dressing casserole you make, Grandma?" Amy asked. "That's not as sloppy as alfredo."

Audrey straightened, smiling. "Yeah! I love that."

Sarah laughed. "I'm sure Pastor John would like it too. I guess we can modify the menu slightly. Let me just check to be sure I have all the ingredients."

At quarter past eleven, the three of them went out to the car. Sarah drove through the snow-lined streets to Pastor John's house on Bridge Street. Audrey hopped out and dashed up the steps to ring the bell while Sarah carefully carried the main course and Amy carried a bag holding a dozen gingersnaps and a small bottle of juice.

"Come on in—it's open," came the reverend's voice from inside, perhaps a little thinner than his usual greeting.

Amy held back inside the doorway. "Is he going to be all...like...banged up?"

"Well, some." Sarah hadn't considered that seeing the pastor bruised and bandaged might be difficult for the girls. "Are you all right?" she whispered. "I know he'll be glad to see you."

Amy nodded, stepping forward to follow Audrey into the living room of the old house.

They found Pastor John leaning back in his recliner. His right arm, heavily bandaged, rested against his chest in a snowy sling, and his right ankle, also wrapped, looked three times the size of his left. Though his color was better than when Sarah had watched him being bundled into the ambulance, he still looked a little pale, and his silver-streaked black hair lay limp over his forehead. On his lap rested an open Bible, two books bristling with bookmarks, a notebook, and several loose papers.

The girls stood staring at the bandages.

"Pardon me for not getting up, ladies," the reverend said with a smile.

"Don't even think of it," Sarah said. "We brought you some lunch."

"That sounds wonderful." Deep creases radiated from the corners of his eyes, and his smile seemed almost a wince.

Sarah looked around for a place to set the plate down and put it on the coffee table a few feet away. "How are you doing? Are you in much pain?"

"I'd be lying if I said no, but thank God, I'm home and able to study some this morning."

"Do you have a folding tray that we can bring over for you to use?"

"Why, yes. In the hall closet." He wriggled in his chair and caught his breath.

"What hurts?" Audrey asked.

He let out a short laugh. "Everything. I'll tell you something, girls. Don't get old."

"Oh, hush," Sarah said. "You aren't old. You're only—what? Fifty-four? Trust me, that's not old. And even young people get injured."

"I suppose so."

"Here, Amy, let's set the cookies and juice on the table too."

Amy held them out, and Sarah took them.

"Oh, cookies!" The pastor's eyes glinted.

"We made them," Audrey said. "Gingersnaps."

"One of my favorites."

"Good, but you have to eat your lunch first," Amy told him solemnly.

"Girls, why don't you go explore the closet in the front hall and find a tray table. Pastor John can use it to hold his books and papers after he eats lunch."

"That would be an improvement," the pastor said with a faint smile. "And I could reach those cookies too."

When the girls left the room, Sarah sat down on the sofa. "How long have you been home?"

"Only an hour or so. Harry brought me."

"Shouldn't you have someone with you today? I thought Eddie Davidson was coming." Sarah noted a folding wheelchair resting in one corner. "You'll need help when you get up."

"Eddie's coming over around supper time. My neighbor is coming to check on me in an hour or so. I'll be fine until then. I feel bad about putting so many people out, though."

Sarah shook her head. "Don't fret. Just concentrate on healing. Martha is doing a wonderful job scheduling volunteers."

"She called a few minutes ago," Pastor John said. "I'm afraid I thought of a few more tasks that should be taken care of. I hated to ask her, but she assured me she'd find someone to fill in and 'be me' this week."

The girls came back with a small folding table. Sarah set it up and positioned it near his recliner. The girls helped put his Bible and papers on it, and Sarah arranged his lunch on a small tray. The pastor moved to raise the back of his recliner and groaned.

Amy pointed to the bottom of his chair. "There's something on the floor."

Audrey stooped and reached under the footrest. "It's your pen." She retrieved it and held it out to him.

"Thank you! I wondered where that had gotten to." He set it carefully beside his Bible. "Amy and Audrey, I wonder if you'd like to do something else to help me."

"Sure," said Audrey.

"Now, don't speak too quickly. It's something that won't be easy."

"What is it?" Amy asked.

"One of the things I especially like to do in the wintertime is to make sure Mrs. Leonard's walk is cleared after we have a snowstorm. She's too frail to do it herself. She has someone come and plow her driveway after it snows, but she doesn't have any family nearby to shovel the walk. So I do that as a way to get exercise and as a kind gesture."

Sarah eyed the girls, wondering how they would respond. At her prompting, they'd done yard work for a widow the summer before, but it hadn't been all fun. "We're in for a big storm tomorrow," she said.

"That's right," said Pastor John. "Now, if you girls are willing, you could be a big blessing to Mrs. Leonard."

"What do you think?" Amy looked expectantly at her sister.

"I don't know." Audrey frowned. "Maybe Amy could shovel and Grandma and I could visit with Mrs. Leonard."

"Hey!" Amy exclaimed. "You'll make me do all the shoveling?"

Pastor John chuckled. "While I do try to visit with Mrs. Leonard every week, it would be a lot of work for just one of you. Maybe you could do the shoveling together."

"Amy's better at that sort of thing," Audrey said.

"What, hard work?" Amy said, and received a sour look from Audrey in return.

"Girls," Sarah interrupted before the girls really started to argue. "Maybe you both could shovel, and both could visit with Mrs. Leonard."

Suddenly Amy found Audrey's arrangement a little more palatable. "I guess I could shovel by myself." She said.

"We'll do it," Audrey said with a nod.

"Are you sure?" he asked.

The girls nodded.

"Thank you, girls. I will feel much better knowing you're taking care of that." The pastor smiled but closed his eyes for a moment.

"Pastor John, is there anything else we can do for you while we're here?" Sarah asked.

"I think I'm all set for now," he said. "Thank you very much."

Sarah smiled at the twins. "We should probably get going, girls. Are you sure you'll be all right until your neighbor arrives?"

"Oh, yes. Thank you so much for coming, and for the meal."

Sarah eyed his bandages again. "Best to take it easy for a while. Let other people take on the load for you. You mustn't be shy about letting us pitch in to help you, when you do so much for other people."

"I guess it's time for me to practice that side of what I preach—letting others have the blessing of helping me."

Sarah picked up her purse and keys. "Now don't you worry about the dishes we brought. I'll pick them up tomorrow after church, and they don't have to be clean when I do." She patted the pastor's sleeve. "Take care."

"Thank you, Sarah. And you too, girls."

"All right, girls," Sarah said. "We have one more stop."

"Yeah, the quilt shop," Audrey said.

Amy rolled her eyes. "It's Wild Goose Chase."

"Actually, we're going to the thrift shop. I don't need to go to the quilt shop today." Sarah herded them toward the door. She had planned to visit the thrift shop on Thursday but with Pastor John's accident that day, she'd never gotten to it.

"Oh boy!" Audrey quickly zipped her jacket. "I got my favorite jumper at the thrift shop."

"Good-bye, Pastor," Sarah called.

"Hey," Amy said as they reached Sarah's car. "Who will shovel Pastor John's walk?"

Sarah ruffled Amy's hair. "That's a very good question, Amy. I think we should drive by after the storm and make sure it's cleared."

On Sunday morning, Sarah and Belle set out for church together in Sarah's car. The snow had not begun yet, but gray clouds made a low, gloomy ceiling of the sky.

"Who's preaching today?" Belle asked.

"I think Martha said the assistant pastor from Cornerstone is coming over this morning."

"Oh, that's good. Poor Pastor John!"

"He was in good spirits yesterday."

When they reached the church, Martha was waiting for Sarah in the narthex. Belle greeted her and left them to sit with a friend.

"Sarah, I've had such a time scheduling people to take over jobs for Pastor John. Since he can't drive, I have to find someone to pick up the missionary who is flying in in a couple of weeks. Hold on," Martha said and made a beeline for an unsuspecting churchgoer.

Sarah waited for her, and a moment later Martha returned, frowning. "I don't enjoy mixing church and business, but it's the easiest time to catch people."

"And hardest for them to say no face to face?" Sarah said.

Martha smiled. "Yes, although so far no one's had problems saying no to a trip to Logan International."

"I'm sure you'll find someone," Sarah said. "There's plenty of time."

"I hope so. You know, Pastor John wanted to come over today, but the deacons convinced him not to try."

"Oh, I certainly am glad to hear that. He's in no condition to try to go anywhere yet." Sarah looked around. "How's Ernie doing?"

"About the same. He's sitting in our usual spot."

"I see him." Sarah smiled. "I'm teaching Angela Miller's class this morning. I'll see you later."

Sarah enjoyed her time with the primary school children. She'd spent the evening before going over the lesson again. They listened as quietly as six- and seven-year-olds could, and answered her questions promptly. Then they made cards for Pastor John, and Sarah promised to deliver them.

After her Sunday school class was dismissed, Audrey ran up to Sarah. Her eyes gleaming, she whispered loudly, "Gram! It's starting to snow!"

The twins still found the New England weather a novelty, having moved to Maple Hill from California the summer before. They'd seen only a couple of respectable storms in December, and Sarah tried to let their excitement override her own apprehension. She didn't mind a good snowstorm. Didn't even mind being snowed in, if she had plenty of supplies and no reason to drive until the roads were cleared. It gave her an excuse to stay home and quilt and read undisturbed—which reminded her of the novel Vanessa had lent her that she hadn't touched yet. But the weatherman's predictions for this storm included at least a foot of snow and warned people to be prepared in case they lost electrical service.

"Maybe you and Amy will be able to go sledding later," she said.

"I hope so! We might even get tomorrow off. Trina says that if it keeps snowing all night, school will be canceled."

"That would be exciting. I'm glad I bought hot chocolate mix and marshmallows."

Audrey's eyes widened. "Oh boy! I love you, Grandma."

Sarah grabbed her hand and squeezed it. "Love you, too."

Audrey hurried to join her parents and Amy a couple of rows behind Martha and Ernie, and Sarah settled in beside them.

"Don't you just love grandchildren?" Martha asked.

"Uh-huh." Sarah took her hymnbook from the rack as one of the deacons walked to the podium.

"I never thought about how much Pastor John does around here until this week," Martha whispered.

"Me either." Sarah glanced up at the board on the side wall, but the hymn numbers hadn't been posted. "Oops, looks like we missed something else."

Martha followed her gaze. "Yes, I thought someone had that job regularly."

Sarah nodded. "Hazel Burkett. She moved away in October. I guess Pastor John's been doing it the last few months."

As the deacon called the number for the last hymn, Martha rummaged in her oversize purse for a notebook and pen to write down the additional task. Sarah quickly found her place in the hymnbook and glanced toward the windows. Snow fell so thick and fast that she could barely see into the parking lot.

After the service, Sarah let Belle take her car home and went with Jason and his family. After they'd stopped at the pastor's house so Sarah could deliver the children's cards, Jason drove to his and Maggie's house. Sarah helped Maggie prepare dinner. Afterward, she spent a couple of hours talking with Jason and Maggie and playing a board game with the girls. At four o'clock, Jason drove her home, following the snowplow until he had to turn onto her street. Sarah got out of the car in front of her garage, waved, and hurried inside. Belle was already settled in before the living room fireplace with a mug of tea and a book.

"Hi," Sarah called as she hung up her coat. "We've got four inches already, and no sign of it letting up. How are you doing?"

"Great. I love blizzards. It's the perfect excuse to be lazy."

Sarah grinned. "I may join you a little later. I want to do some quilting first."

She took out the two flannel shirts she'd bought at the thrift shop and spent a half hour carefully cutting as many full squares as possible from them for Vern's quilt. With a few pieces from her leftover fabric and what she'd bought at Vanessa's store, she had a pleasing pattern. The embellishments would be added to some of the squares next. She pulled together the scraps of shirts and examined the pockets, plackets, and cuffs for pieces sturdy enough to use.

The softness of the fabric and the colorful squares gave her a feeling of comfort and warmth. Now that she had the layout planned, she could envision the exact shades she wanted for the borders. She'd need a couple of yards of a bright flannel—red and green if she could get it—for the strips, as well as batting and a coordinating sheet for the backing.

It was after six o'clock when she realized she'd neglected her boarder. She found Belle in the kitchen, scouting the contents of the refrigerator.

"I feel as though I should eat something," Sarah said, "but I'm not very hungry. Maggie served lasagna for lunch."

"I could make omelets," Belle offered.

Sarah stepped aside. "If you want to cook omelets, I won't say no. I'll set the table and fix a salad."

When they'd eaten and cleaned up, both women drifted back to the living room.

Sarah brought out her library book about the Pacific battles. Maybe she could finish the section on the Guadalcanal campaign, and then she could get to the book Vanessa had lent her. She sat down before the fire while Belle added a couple of logs to the blaze.

"That's awfully heavy reading, isn't it?" Belle pushed back her short blonde curls and went to the sofa.

Belle was right. Sarah looked over at the book Vanessa had lent her—*Before the Storm* by Marjory Middlefield.

Perhaps a novel would be a little bit more cozy as a fireside read. She picked it up and opened to the first few pages. She knew from the cover that it wouldn't be a medieval romance, but she was surprised to find the opening scene happening in New England in the late thirties in the midst of a snow-storm.

She settled into her chair and began to read.

CHAPTER SIX

Looking out the window Monday morning, Sarah told herself not to expect to hear from Laura Baird that day. About a foot and a half of snow had accumulated in the front yard. If Concord had gotten as much as Maple Hill, the public library there would probably stay closed for the day.

Belle came into the kitchen smiling ruefully. "I called my boss, and she said not to come in today. She figures business will be slow, so I get a vacation. Guess I don't have an excuse not to do my laundry and thoroughly clean my room. It really needs it."

Sarah laughed. "You must be exaggerating. You're one of my neater boarders!"

"Not by much. It will be nice to have a whole day off, though."

The young man who plowed the driveway for Sarah wouldn't come until the snowfall ended. Since she couldn't go out, she determined to make the most of the morning.

After some light housework downstairs, she went to her sewing room and worked on Vern's quilt, pinning the "extras" she'd selected to half a dozen of the squares. On a whim, she cut the tags out of what remained of the shirts' collars and set them aside to add to the quilt top later. She wondered how Pastor John was doing. About ten o'clock, she took a tea break and called John's cell phone. He answered right away.

"I'm doing fine, Sarah. Thanks for checking on me. One of the deacons is shoveling my front steps right now."

Late that afternoon, after getting a good start on sewing the quilt squares together, Sarah checked her e-mail. A message in her in-box made her lean forward eagerly.

Mrs. Hart, I'm working at home today because of the storm, but Saturday I brought home the high school annuals for the years you inquired about. Here are the results I've found pertinent to your question: I found one Robert Willis who graduated from Concord High School during the time period you asked about (1942), and two young women named Joan (1939 and 1942). I also found a Vern Pickett listed as an underclassman in the 1941 yearbook and previous years. But alas, he does not show up as a senior with his class in the 1942 annual. Is it possible that this student transferred to another school before his senior year? Alice Ward was also a member of the 1942 class. Feel free to telephone me at home if you have any questions. Laura Baird.

Sarah's adrenaline surged. She was on the right path. Below the closing was a telephone number, and she reached eagerly for her phone. Laura answered on the second ring, and Sarah quickly identified herself.

"Thank you so much for contacting me today. I didn't expect you to work on this at home."

"I'm happy to help you," Laura said. "Sometimes I'll take a project home over the weekend, and with the snowy forecast, it seemed like an especially good idea this week. Did the information I sent answer your questions?"

"Partly." Sarah smiled grimly as she reread the e-mail she'd printed out. "I'm afraid it also raised some new ones."

"That's often the case. If there's anything I can do on this end, I'd be happy to help."

"You see, Vern Pickett is the one who started me on this adventure," Sarah said. "He's in his eighties now, and he'd like to find his old classmates, but especially Alice Ward. I'm surprised he didn't tell me that he didn't graduate from Concord High. The last time I talked to him, I specifically asked him about graduation years so that your search would be easier, and his memory seemed to have failed him a little. I thought it was strange that he couldn't tell me what year he and his friends had graduated."

"That is a bit odd," Laura said. "Still, if he didn't graduate with them, it's a little more understandable. And after all, it was almost seventy years ago. That's a long time."

"Yes." Sarah opened the notebook she'd given over to Vern's case. "You may be right about him transferring for his last year. I'll have to talk to him again when this storm is over."

"If you think it would help, I can read you the entries under the students' photos in their senior annual."

"Would you? I'd appreciate that." Sarah waited while Laura found the appropriate pages.

"Here's Robert Willis. Nickname, Bob. He was on the track and basketball teams and the yearbook staff. And for most of the students, they listed future plans. It seems Bob planned to enlist in the Army Air Corps after graduation."

"I wonder if he came back to Concord after the war," Sarah mused as she jotted down the information. Her mind leaped to all sorts of possibilities. If she couldn't find Bob in or near Concord, she might be able to find some other men who had played on the basketball team with him. "What about the girls?"

"Well, let's see. Alice Ward, no nickname given. She was a member of the debate team and the chorus. She graduated magna cum laude and planned to go to Radcliffe College."

"Wonderful." Sarah breathed out a sigh of satisfaction. Finally, something solid about Alice. "Now, you said there were two Joans, and one was in Alice's class."

"Yes. Let me find it. ..." Sarah heard the rustle of turning pages. "Here we go. Joan Franklin. Nickname, Jo. Aha. She was also in the chorus, and she was in the French club. Oh, this will interest you."

"What?" Sarah asked, her pen poised to write.

"Joan Franklin also planned to go to Radcliffe."

A few minutes later, Sarah and Laura ended their conversation. Sarah searched right away for a Radcliffe College alumnae site. To her delight, she found a listing of interviews with several members of the class of 1946. However, neither Alice Ward nor Joan Franklin was listed among them. Another false start. But the new data Laura had provided still gave her hope.

"Grandma!" Audrey and Amy tumbled through the backdoor and into Sarah's kitchen on Tuesday afternoon.

"Stand still," Maggie called as she entered behind them. "Don't go off the mat in your wet boots."

Sarah hurried to them, smiling. "Don't worry about a little snow on this floor. It will wipe up easily." She hugged the twins and then her daughter-in-law.

"So, you had two whole days off from school," she said to the girls.

"Yes, and guess where we've been?"

Sarah glanced out the window. "I can't imagine."

"We went to Mrs. Leonard's," Amy said as she pulled off her blue and white mittens.

"That's right—you promised Pastor John you'd shovel her walk when the storm ended." Sarah looked over the girls' heads as they stooped to pull off their boots.

Maggie nodded, smiling. "They did a terrific job."

"Yeah, and afterward—" Audrey yanked off her right boot. "We built a snowman in her yard."

"A snowman?" Sarah laughed. "What fun!"

"Yeah. It's the first one we ever made." Amy set her boots on the plastic drip tray Sarah kept near the kitchen door in winter, and straightened to remove her scarf and jacket. "*That* part was fun. The shoveling part was hard. We built the snowman where she can see it out her window, when she's sitting in her rocking chair."

"She loved it," Audrey added. "Even if it was kind of crooked."

"What's not to love?" Sarah asked.

Maggie grinned. "I had fun working on the snowman too. It's been years and years since I've been where there was enough snow to do that."

"And you know what?" Amy asked.

"What?" Sarah reveled in the twins' enthusiasm.

"When we finished, she stood at the window and motioned for us to come in." Amy beckoned with her arm.

Audrey unzipped her jacket. "She had candy canes for us."

Amy leaned toward Sarah with an impish smile. "I think they were left over from Christmas."

"Now, girls, candy canes keep a *long* time." Maggie took Audrey's jacket and hung it on a hook.

"Oh, they tasted fine," Amy said.

"Well, it sounds as if you had quite an afternoon. Can you come in and sit by the fireplace for a little while? My teakettle's hot."

The four of them were soon seated in front of the fire with steaming mugs in hand. Maggie and Sarah sipped spiced tea while the twins enjoyed hot chocolate with marshmallows.

"I didn't open the store today," Maggie said. "It wouldn't have made sense. Nobody would have come in, anyway, and with the girls off from school, I decided to take another full day off."

"Day off?" Audrey said. "Mom, you spent all morning cleaning."

Maggie shrugged. "I'd let a lot of things go the last couple of weeks. It was good to catch up on some of them. Although it would be nice sometime to have a day when I can just relax."

Sarah knew starting the store had been a struggle— Maggie had worked nonstop since she and Jason had moved to Maple Hill last summer, first to restore their Victorian house, and then to build her antiques business. Her penchant for overachieving had caused a little strain in the family, and Sarah suspected the girls were glad to have her home for a couple of days, even if it involved work at home.

"What did you do, Grandma?" Amy asked. "Did you shovel your driveway?"

Sarah smiled. "No, I hire a man to come and plow it for me. It was a perfect day for quilting, though. I got a lot done. Let me show you how Mr. Pickett's quilt is coming." She got up and fetched the flannel quilt top.

"It looks a lot like Grandpa's," Audrey said.

"It's very much like it. Today I sewed the squares together. I still need to do a couple more rows of squares, put the border on, baste the top to the backing, and quilt it."

"That's a lot of work," Amy said.

Sarah spread the quilt over the coffee table, and the girls reached out to touch the soft material. "This red and black square with the pocket in the middle is from one of Mr. Pickett's old shirts. That green plaid one is from another. See? I put three pockets on the quilt. If he wants to put a handkerchief in there to keep it handy, he can."

"Or his TV remote," Audrey suggested.

They all laughed.

"This is wonderful, Sarah," Maggie said. "He's going to love it."

"I hope so. I'm going to machine quilt it. They go together so easily, it hardly seems like work."

"Can I help?" Audrey asked.

"Maybe. I have some leftover material from the borders for this one, and a few extra squares. I was thinking maybe I'd make a matching pillow sham." Sarah looked over at Amy, but she seemed focused on spooning the remains of her marshmallow out of her cocoa.

"We could help you tomorrow," Audrey said, bouncing a little on the sofa.

"Easy, honey. You'll spill your cocoa." Maggie arched her eyebrows until Audrey sat still again. "Besides, you'll have school tomorrow."

"Aw. I was hoping for another day off," Amy said.

"Me too." Audrey sipped her hot chocolate.

Maggie shook her head and grinned. "No, I'm pretty sure they'll have all the roads cleared by morning. And I'll open the antique shop. Even if business is slow in January, there's a lot I need to do at the store."

"Maybe you girls can come here after school," Sarah said. "I won't start the pillow sham until you can be here to help. And, Amy, if you want to do something else, you can."

"I might help you. We'll see."

Sarah nodded. It pleased her that the girls showed some interest in crafts. Audrey especially had an artistic bent, but Amy preferred sports to handwork. Anything that would allow her to spend time with the girls was a bonus, though. She looked to Maggie. "Do you think the school would let the bus driver drop them here if you wrote a note?"

"Maybe. Are you sure you want these hooligans here?"

"Sure. I could give them supper and take them back to you that evening."

Maggie nodded slowly.

"What's this?" Amy held up a paperback book she'd discovered on the end table.

"Oh, that's a novel Mrs. Sawyer lent me," Sarah said. "She wanted me to read something by her favorite author. I've barely started it, but it's interesting."

After Maggie and the girls had left, Sarah decided to go and talk to Vern. She'd planned to wait until his quilt was finished, but now she had some questions for him, and she didn't want to put off getting the answers any longer than necessary.

She pulled on her fleece-lined boots, mentally reviewing what she'd learned from the librarian in Concord. She wanted to explore Vern's fractured memories of high school and Alice. What had Alice meant to him then? And would the information Laura had found stir his memories?

She drove slowly through the snowy streets. Everywhere, high snow banks were shoved into the corners of parking lots. A front-end loader working near the Green scooped up snow and plopped it into a dump truck to be hauled out of the center of town. If another storm came along with all that snow piled up, they'd have trouble clearing the streets, so the custom was to haul it away and dump it in an out-of-the-way spot.

As Sarah drove up the knoll to Bradford Manor, the low rays of the sun glittered on the new snow. An image of a winter quilt popped into her head. White squares with triangles of various greens, representing the conifers, and slashes of orange and red to make a spectacular sunset. She sighed. So many quilt ideas, so little time.

She went to her father's room first. He was napping, so she left her coat there and went on down the hall to find Vern. McKenna and Caleb were visiting him.

"Hello, Mrs. Hart," McKenna said as she entered. "We stopped by to see if Grandpa was getting cabin fever from the snowstorm."

Vern chuckled. "More likely you two were the ones antsy to get out. How are you, Sarah?"

"I'm fine," Sarah said. "I wanted to talk to you about Alice Ward again. Is this a good time?"

"It's as good as any, I guess."

Sarah looked from him to McKenna. She ought to have called first. Her father didn't like to talk on the phone, so she dropped in on him without notice once or twice a week. But Vern might not be comfortable with that.

He held out a plastic box of oatmeal cookies. "McKenna brought some treats. Care to join us?"

"Thank you. Those look delicious."

McKenna moved out of the extra chair so Sarah could have it and sat on Vern's bed. "Come here, Caleb. Want to climb up on Grandpa's bed? Oh, be careful of your cookie."

"Too late," Vern said, as the little boy's cookie hit the floor.

"I'll take care of it. Excuse me." McKenna picked up the half-eaten cookie and squeezed past Sarah to Vern's bathroom.

Sarah doubted Vern would be able to pull out any fresh details for her with the rambunctious toddler visiting. Maybe she should come back at a quieter time.

"Did you find out something?" Vern asked.

"Well, yes and no. A little bit. The librarian in Concord looked at some old high school yearbooks. She found Bob Willis in the 1942 annual."

"That's right. Bob was a good student."

"Yes. But not as good as Alice, right?"

"She was always studying." His brown eyes flicked to Caleb and back.

"She graduated with highest honors."

"What else?"

Sarah frowned. "Does the name Joan Franklin mean anything to you?"

Vern's brow puckered. "Franklin...Franklin. Hmm."

"Joan Franklin was in your class. She and Alice both sang in the school's chorus. I think she's the one you mentioned to me, who was Alice's best friend."

"Could be," he said.

Sarah was disappointed that he couldn't confirm her hunch. Vern seemed less in touch today than during their previous conversations. Why hadn't the information she'd brought sparked further memories?

Caleb toddled over and grabbed the strap of Sarah's purse. She let him tug on it, but held the bag firmly on her lap. "Well, there was another girl named Joan, but she graduated in 1939. I figured she was too old to be Alice's friend."

"You're probably right."

McKenna came out of the bathroom with a damp paper towel. She dabbed at the carpet, where Caleb's gooey cookie had fallen.

Sarah looked over at Vern. He was gazing at Caleb, who now crawled on all fours between Vern's wheelchair and the dresser.

"Be careful, Caleb. You don't want to get stuck back there," he said.

McKenna was just returning from throwing away the paper towel. "I'm sorry, Grandpa. Why don't I take him for a walk down to the lobby, to see the birds? That will give you and Mrs. Hart a few minutes' peace."

"Thank you," Sarah said with a smile. "I won't stay long—I know Vern enjoys seeing his little great-grandson."

"I sure do," Vern said.

When they had left the room, it seemed very quiet. "He's a handsome little fellow," Sarah said. "I think he's going to have the Pickett nose."

"The—oh, sure." Vern laughed and touched his own slightly long nose. "It's not too bad, but it is distinctive."

"Did you write anything down for me?" Sarah asked.

"Did I . . . oh, no, I guess I forgot. Sorry."

Sarah took that as a matter of course. "Well, about graduation."

"Yes?" He focused on her, his brown eyes wide behind his glasses.

"You didn't graduate with your class, did you, Vern?"

"Wh-what?"

"You weren't in the senior annual with the rest of your class—Bob Willis and your other classmates. You were in the juniors' section in the book the previous year, but not in the 1942 senior yearbook. Did you leave Concord? I thought maybe you'd transferred to another school. Did you move away?"

"N-no."

Sarah tried to puzzle that out. "Did you drop out, then?"

"I . . ." Vern turned away from her. "You know, my memory isn't so good. I'm sorry, but I just can't recall the details.

Graduation and all that. Maybe I just didn't get my picture done like the others. We didn't have much money. My family probably couldn't afford it."

She sat in silence for a long moment. She had assumed he'd graduated with Alice in 1942 and then enlisted, but maybe not. She didn't like causing him stress. A pang of guilt nudged her. She didn't want to upset him. Yet, if he really wanted to find Alice, she'd have to probe further. "Graduation is a big milestone in a young person's life," she said. "It's all right to tell me if you didn't graduate. But if you did, it seems you'd remember it. Do you have a diploma? Or maybe you got a certificate after the war?"

He shook his head. "You know what? I don't really feel like talking about this anymore."

Sarah stood, feeling she'd failed in her mission. The only thing she'd accomplished was making Vern feel sad.

"I'm sorry. I'll see if I can find out anything more, and I'll get back to you."

"All right." He didn't look at her as she walked toward the door.

CHAPTER SEVEN

Sarah drove to the church on Wednesday morning, though she'd planned to stay home and work on Vern's quilt and the mystery of Alice. A call from Angela Miller had reminded her that she needed to return the Sunday school teaching materials, and Angela had suggested she leave them off at the church, since she lived several miles out of town but would be in Maple Hill later that day.

Sarah stopped first at Pastor John's house to get the key to the side door and leave him a couple of blueberry muffins.

"How's the ankle doing?" she asked.

"It's still sore, but they tell me that's normal. If you ladies keep feeding me this well and I can't get any exercise, I'm going to get fat." The pastor's twinkling eyes belied his complaint, and Sarah chuckled.

"Oh, you! Just behave yourself and get better." She took the key and drove on to the church. The parking lot had been plowed, and she noted that the small amount of snow on the pavement was crunchy, not slippery. The deacons had made liberal use of rock salt to melt the ice after the pastor's fall.

She unlocked the door and pulled it open. A wave of warm air flowed over her. That surprised her—the part-time secretary must be at work on the bulletins. But when she reached the door to the church office, she found it was locked. She unbuttoned her coat and walked up the stairs to the sanctuary. The air was even warmer on the upper level, and she pulled her hat off. At the thermostat on the wall in the entry, she squinted at the numbers.

"Oh dear." The thermometer showed seventy-four. She turned the dial back to sixty-five degrees.

She left the Sunday school packet where she'd agreed to and hurried back out to her car. The key had to go back to the pastor's house, and she told John she'd found the heat on. "Do you know whose job it is to turn it down in the church after services?"

Pastor John raised his hand. "That would be me. I never gave it a thought. Since I'm usually the last one out, I turn the thermostat down when I leave."

"It's not a problem," Sarah said. "We'll make sure some-one takes care of it."

"I'm about as useful as a slug."

"Now, stop that. You know the Lord was right there when you fell. We don't know why, but this is all part of his plan for you—and for us."

"I expect you're right, Sarah. Forgive me for com-plaining."

She smiled down at him. "Oh, don't think about it. It's reassuring to know you're human."

"Well, right now I wish I were superhuman."

As she drove away, Sarah mulled over the incident and decided she'd better stop at Martha's.

"Doesn't one of the trustees do that?" Martha let out a heavy sigh after Sarah had told her what had happened. "I guess you wouldn't be here if they did."

"It's not a big deal," Sarah said. "It's just that no one remembered on Sunday."

"All that wasted energy to heat an empty church," Martha moaned.

"Martha, honey, you can't worry about all these things. Just take them one at a time, and keep on doing what you're doing—ask other people to help. It's all you can do. I told John we'd speak to the trustees, and if you want me to call—"

"I'll do it," Martha said. "And I'll put it on my chart. I've got quite a list of jobs the pastor was doing that have to be done by someone else while he's laid up. I sure didn't realize how much he did."

"Me either. Are you sure this isn't too much for you?"

"No, I'm doing all right. It's more involved than I thought it would be, but I think things are under control."

"Good. I'm sure it's most efficient to have one person listing the jobs and assigning them. You're doing great."

"Thanks."

Sarah heard a plaintive note in her friend's usually cheerful voice. "Is everything all right?"

"Oh, I don't know." Martha looked quickly over her shoulder and lowered her voice. "Ernie's having a not-so-good day."

Since Ernie was diagnosed with Parkinson's disease the summer before, the couple had learned to cope, but some days were more trying than others. The worst days happened when Ernie let his illness and the occasional tremor he'd developed frustrate him.

"I'm sorry," Sarah said. "Can you take time out for a cup of tea?"

Martha smiled at her. "If you'll fix it while I call the head trustee. I don't want to forget."

"I'd be happy to. Shall I fix a cup for Ernie too?"

"I'll ask him."

Martha left the room, and Sarah filled the teakettle and put it on the stove. She knew her way around Martha's kitchen as well as she did her own. She opened a cupboard and took out a selection of tea bags.

The kettle was just beginning to boil when Martha returned. "There. The heat problem is taken care of. Ernie's sitting in his recliner, and he says he'd like to have some tea in there. Just don't make it too hot in case he spills a little. I'll take it to him."

Martha took a clean dish towel from a drawer and carried Ernie's tea to the living room. Sarah took their mugs to the table and sat down.

"What can I do to help you?" she asked when Martha returned. "Do you need more meals for Pastor John?"

"No, I've got the next few days covered for food. I still haven't found a driver to pick up the missionary speaker the first week in February, but first things first."

Martha retrieved a notebook and brought it to the table. She closed her eyes briefly as she opened it. "I hate to ask you this, because I know you're busy, and you're already doing a lot...."

"What?" Sarah asked. "Anything I can do to help you, I'll do."

"Saturday is food pantry day."

"Oh, and Pastor John is usually there."

"Right. He and a couple of volunteers."

"I can do it." Sarah mentally pictured her anticipated schedule for Saturday. She had toyed with a drive to Concord, but she didn't have anything specific to investigate there yet. The quilting and researching she probably would have worked on could be shuffled to other times. "Yes, it will work out well for me."

"Thank you. Belle is signed up to help," Martha said, "so I thought the two of you might work well together, and you could drive over together. And Harry Butler will be there. We always like to have a man to move the cases of food around."

"It should work out perfectly." Sarah said. "We'll be there, ready to serve."

Martha sighed and jotted Sarah's name on her chart. "Thanks. Just when I think I've got everything covered, I learn about some new job that needs to be done. It was hard

to get anyone to shovel the steps at church and the area outside the side entrance yesterday, after the storm. Everyone
had their own snow to get rid of."

"Well, it's beautifully done now. And someone shoveled
Pastor John's walkway for him."

Martha nodded. "I think Jason did that this morning."

Sarah sipped her tea. "Well, I think you're doing the
work of about three people yourself. Just check off the food
pantry. If a problem comes up with Belle or Harry, I'll find
someone else to be there Saturday. You relax and take care
of Ernie. And yourself."

Since Amy and Audrey were coming after school, Sarah had
time to make only one call concerning Vern's mystery.

She had hoped to contact some of the Willises in Concord earlier, but hadn't gotten to it. Now she opened her
notebook to the list of phone numbers she had copied there
and punched in the first one.

"Hello?" The voice sounded like that of a teenage boy.

Sarah cleared her throat. "Hello. My name is Sarah Hart.
I'm looking for a gentleman named Bob Willis, who lived
in Concord many years ago, or for any members of Bob's
family."

"I don't know a Bob," the young man said.

"Oh. Well, he would be in his eighties now, and I'm not
even sure that he's still living. Do you know of any elderly
folks named Willis living in the Concord area?"

"There're my grandparents, James and Dorothy Willis."

Sarah looked quickly down her list and spotted a listing for a James Willis. "Is their number by any chance—" She read it off.

"Yup, that's it."

"Thank you for your help."

As soon as she'd hung up, Sarah went to the front window and peered out. The school bus was pulling up at the end of her driveway. Amy and Audrey bounded off, and Audrey turned to wave to someone on the bus.

Sarah met them at the door and welcomed them into her warm kitchen.

"Are we going to sew today?" Amy asked.

"We sure are. Snack first, then we'll get at it."

Sarah set out a plate of cookies and poured a glass of milk for each of the girls. She joined them and asked them about school while they ate.

"It's okay," said Audrey, "but Mrs. Jefferson keeps calling me Amy."

"Wonder why." Amy rolled her eyes.

Sarah chuckled. "I guess you two are used to that."

"Yeah, but we don't even sit together. Why can't she just learn which one's near the door and which one's in the middle of the room?" Audrey reached for another cookie.

"And wearing outfits that are nothing alike doesn't help?" Sarah asked. Amy had on jeans and a plaid blouse, while Audrey wore green corduroy pants with a matching vest and cream-colored shirt.

"Apparently not," Amy said. "I think it's partly because our names both start with A. Maybe you should use your middle name."

"Marie?" Audrey scowled at her. "Who wants to be called Marie?"

Amy shrugged. "Well, when we're grown up, we can change our names, I guess."

"The names won't matter then," Audrey said.

"You've got a point there." Sarah set down her teacup. "When you're grown, people probably won't see you together nearly as often, and chances are you'll have different last names."

"I like Hart," Amy said.

"Me too. I'm keeping it." Audrey drained her milk glass.

"Well, if you're both ready, shall we go into the sewing room?" Sarah rose and led the way, reflecting how much things could change between the ages of twelve and twenty.

"Here are the squares for Mr. Pickett's pillow sham."

"Wow, you already cut them all out." Audrey fingered a couple of four-inch squares Sarah had cut from the best shirt McKenna had given her.

"These are from one we got at the thrift shop Saturday," said Amy, reaching for another pile.

Sarah put her hands on her hips. "How did you get such a fabulous memory, young lady? It certainly wasn't from my side of the family. Those did come from the thrift shop, and this pile is from the leftovers of the fabric I used for the border around Mr. Pickett's quilt. Now, our design is a plain one—just squares—but you know men like things simple and practical. Most men, that is. Oh, they like pretty things, too, but usually not frilly things."

"How did Grandpa like his quilt?" Audrey asked.

Sarah smiled. "I think he likes it a lot. When I visited him yesterday, he had it spread over him."

"That's nice," Amy said.

Sarah nodded. "People Grandpa William's age don't need much, and it's hard sometimes to think of a good gift for someone like that. But a quilt is useful and beautiful."

"Well, he liked the candy we gave him for his birthday too," Amy said. "He gave us a piece before we left."

Audrey frowned. "I don't know if he liked the bathrobe Mom picked out."

"I'm sure he'll use it." Sarah said. "All right, why don't you each lay out a row of six squares any way you think looks nice. We'll pin them together and see if they look good next to each other. We'll stitch them on the sewing machine, into long strips, and then we'll put those together."

The girls shuffled the squares for several minutes, trying the effects of the different plaids next to each other. At last they were satisfied and pinned them together.

By quarter to five, they had finished the front of the pillow sham, and Sarah had showed them how she gathered the red fabric that would form the ruffle.

"Now all I have to do is sew that on and put the back on," she said as they put away the sewing supplies. "Thanks for your help, girls. Do you have any homework?"

"We have some reading to do for science, and we have to write a character sketch for English."

"You'd better get busy while I get supper."

Sarah hummed as she heated slices of ham and made a salad. Having Jason, Maggie, and the girls close by was a blessing she never stopped giving thanks for. They'd made some big adjustments, and she knew they'd done it in part for her. But with them close at hand, she wasn't nearly as lonely as she'd been in the first few years after her husband Gerry died. Her daughter Jenna lived thousands of miles away in Texas, and for the most part Sarah's contact with her was confined to frequent e-mails and telephone calls, though the family had flown to Massachusetts for Thanksgiving.

On a whim, she went to the hutch and took out three of her best china plates. Belle would be late tonight and wouldn't be home for supper. Sarah wanted to make the occasion festive for the twins, even though the food would be plain. She sent up a prayer of thanksgiving as she lifted down three of the goblets she used only on special occasions.

On the way home after dropping the girls off, Sarah mentally replayed her day. Her time with Amy and Audrey had been sheer delight. She'd have Vern's quilt ready to give him soon. She still wondered about his graduation—or lack thereof. The more she thought about it, the more convinced she was that his family hadn't moved, and he hadn't transferred to another school. The only thing that made sense to her was that he couldn't remember the year of his graduation because he'd never graduated. Was he ashamed of that? And had he dropped out of school to join the war effort? A lot of young men had.

When she got home, Belle was nowhere in sight, but the dishwasher was running. Sarah smiled, knowing her model boarder had cleaned up after her own evening meal and run the load of dishes Sarah had left.

She decided it wasn't too late to call over to the Pickett house—only eight-thirty. Scott hadn't been very helpful at first, but he'd come around. She hadn't known what to ask him then. Maybe she knew enough now to stir up what he did know about his grandfather.

His upbeat "Hello, Mrs. Hart. What's up?" brought a smile to her face.

"Scott, do you know if your grandfather actually graduated from high school?"

He hesitated. "Well, sure. I mean, Concord High and the blue Chevy, and all that."

"But the librarian in Concord told me that Vern doesn't have a senior picture in the high school yearbook the year he should have graduated. When I asked him about it, your grandfather seemed to have a very poor memory about that subject. Now I'm wondering if he was just embarrassed to tell me he never finished school."

"You mean . . . he dropped out?"

"Possibly. What do you think?"

"I don't know. I always assumed he graduated. He did say he joined the army not long after Pearl Harbor."

Sarah nodded. "See, that's what I'm talking about. According to the previous yearbooks, Vern should have graduated with the class of 1942. But he didn't. Or if he did, his photo and all mention of him got left out of the yearbook."

"That's kind of weird," Scott said.

"My thought exactly."

"Well…is it important?"

"I'm not sure," Sarah said. "If it's not, then why didn't he just tell me?"

"I guess I should know more about the family's history. I like Grandpa a lot, but I never paid a lot of attention to that stuff."

A new thought hit Sarah. "Didn't Vern have any siblings? He's not an only child, is he?"

"One sister. Aunt Nora. She lives in Arizona."

"Is she older than Vern, or younger?"

"Uh…older, I think. I'm not sure."

"When was the last time she visited?" Sarah asked.

"I don't know. I've never met Aunt Nora."

Sarah drew in a sharp breath. "Not once?"

"No." Scott sounded apologetic and a little embarrassed. "Grandpa used to talk about going down to visit her, but he never did that I can remember. Maybe when he was younger. I know she hasn't been here within my memory— say, twenty or twenty-five years. But Grandpa gets a

Christmas card from her every year. When she had a heart operation, he talked about flying down, but he didn't do it."

Sarah decided now wasn't the time to express how odd she found that. "Thank you, Scott. I appreciate your help."

She hung up and took out the picture of Alice again. Looking into the pretty girl's face didn't give her any brilliant ideas.

"Alice," she said aloud, "for someone who wants to find you, Vern Pickett is making my job awfully hard."

The next morning, Sarah sat down with her notebook and telephone, determined to make a breakthrough on Vern's case. Not all of these young people's families could have pulled up stakes and left Concord. She began with the number for James and Dorothy Willis.

"Hello?" The woman sounded mature. Sarah introduced herself and explained what she was looking for.

"So I wondered if you knew or were possibly related to Bob Willis, who lived in Concord back in the nineteen forties."

"Sure, I knew Bob."

Sarah was thankful she had sat down. She couldn't believe she had finally found someone from Vern's past.

"I'm Dorothy Willis," the woman said. "Bob was my husband's uncle. But he passed away a few years ago."

Sarah tried not to feel frustrated. At least she had found someone who had known Bob. "I'm sorry. I don't know much about Bob, but I found out he graduated from Concord High School in 1942, and at that time his plans were to join the Air Force. That is, the Army Air Corps."

"Oh, he did," Dorothy said. "He served with distinction in the war. He was over in England, flying out over France and Germany—one of those hotshot aces. Came home a hero, and he always wore his uniform in the Memorial and Veterans Day parades, as long as he was able. We were all proud of him."

Sarah jotted in her notebook. On a hunch, she said, "I don't suppose you'd know of a woman named Joan—I think her last name was Franklin—who would have been about Bob's age. I believe they were in school together."

"Hmm, you'll have to ask my husband that one," Dorothy said. "It's beyond what little I know."

A moment later, a man came on the phone. "Hello. James Willis here."

"Hello, Mr. Willis. My name is Sarah Hart, and I live over in Maple Hill. I'm trying to track down some old classmates of a friend, and I understand you were related to Bob Willis."

"Oh sure. But Uncle Bob's been gone awhile."

"Would you happen to know any other people he went to school with? I'm especially looking for Alice Ward and Joan Franklin."

"Hmm. Tell you what: The person you really want to talk to is my cousin Carl. Bob was his father, and if anyone can tell you about his old friends, it would be Carl."

"Wonderful. Do you have a number for Carl? I'd love to speak to him."

James gave her his cousin's home telephone number. "He's over at the office most days. He's semiretired, but he still goes in a lot."

"Thank you so much, Mr. Willis." Sarah hung up feeling she had found another solid lead. It was too bad Vern's old buddy had passed away, but she felt significantly closer to finding out what had happened to Alice.

The woman who answered her call to Carl's home told her to phone the office. Sarah went to the kitchen and quickly fixed herself a cup of tea. Explaining her motives and her mission to one person after another drained her. With the mug of strong, black tea steaming nearby, she punched in the next number. A helpful receptionist transferred her call to Carl Willis's office.

"Joan Franklin? Yes, she still lives in town. But she's Joan Nash now."

Sarah's heart leaped. "Mr. Willis, if you could help me locate her, I'd be very grateful. She was also good friends with another girl named Alice Ward," Sarah said.

"Huh. I don't recall that name."

Sarah sighed. Well, at least she was one step closer. "Did your father ever speak of a friend named Vern Pickett?"

"Land, yes. Many times. Dad used to talk about the stunts they pulled when they were kids. Vern was from the wrong side of the tracks, so to speak. Poor family. But my dad liked him."

"This Joan Franklin Nash you mentioned..."

"Yes. She's married to Donald Nash. I think they're in the phone book. Let me see..."

A minute later, Sarah hung up. She felt she was close. Very close. She took a big sip of tea and picked up the phone again. She couldn't help but wish she were in Concord, interviewing these people face to face.

"Joan Nash," said a bright, feminine voice.

"Hello." Sarah quickly gave her spiel to identify herself and explain her quest. "Carl Willis thought you might be able to help me."

Joan chuckled. "Sounds like Carl. Just because I used to work at the information center, he thinks I know everything about Concord."

Sarah noted the slight tremor in the woman's voice, even though she seemed cheerful. "I'm trying to help an old friend, Mrs. Nash. Do you know a gentleman named Vern Pickett?"

After a significant pause, Joan said with a bit of a huff, "Well, *I knew* Vern, but I'm not sure he was a gentleman."

"Oh?" Sarah wasn't sure what to say next, but Mrs. Nash saved her the trouble.

"He treated my best friend very shabbily."

Sarah let out her pent-up breath. "Oh, dear. I'm sorry. I've been looking very hard for a clue to the whereabouts of his old schoolmates, and this is the first solid result I've had."

"You talk as though Vern's alive," Joan said. "As if you know him."

"I do. Vern is very much alive, and I'm sure he'd love to connect with you again."

"Is that right? I'm not sure I'd want to see him."

"Oh." Sarah gulped. "Even more, there's someone else he'd like to know about. I've just learned that his dear friend Bob Willis has passed away, but I would be so happy if I could tell him that Alice Ward is still on this earth."

"Oh my." Sarah thought she heard a sniff. Joan said softly, "If you learn it's true, I do hope you'll tell me too. Alice was my dearest friend during high school, but in the late nineteen forties, Alice and I completely lost touch."

CHAPTER EIGHT

Sarah woke Friday morning feeling dissatisfied. Her clock told her she'd slept a little later than usual. She sat up and looked toward the window. No wonder. The short January days were dim enough, but this dawning was grayer than most. Snow fell in big, fluffy flakes. She hoped it wouldn't last. January weather had hampered her plans enough already.

As she dressed, she remembered her conversation with Joan Nash. Her most promising lead in the Alice Ward quest had turned into another dead end. Joan hadn't heard from her friend for more than sixty years.

A quick check on the Concord library's schedule motivated her to put her sleuthing skills in neutral for a while until they opened. She fixed breakfast and saw Belle off to work, then spent an hour working on Vern's quilt. At least her gift might soften the blow of her news when she told him she hadn't found Alice.

Promptly at nine, she called the distant library.

"Still looking for the class of '42?" Laura Baird asked with a chuckle.

"Well, I found one of them. Joan Franklin is now Joan Nash, and she's still living right there in Concord."

"Oh, I think I remember Mrs. Nash. She used to come into the library often, back before she retired from working at the information center. It never occurred to me that she was one of the students you were looking for."

"Well, I learned that Bob Willis passed away. But I still haven't gotten a line on Alice Ward. Joan lost touch with her ages ago."

"Hmm. I'm guessing you've thought of a new approach."

Sarah smiled. "That's right. Vern has a sister, Nora Pickett. She's still living, but she's very frail, and she lives in Arizona. I assume she went to the public schools in Concord too."

"I can certainly check on her if you think that will help. You want to know if she graduated, even though her brother didn't, is that it?"

"Yes." Sarah appreciated the way Laura leaped to her own mental wavelength. "The family may have moved away, but the most likely possibility is that Vern's military service interrupted his schooling."

"Did you ask him?"

"Yes, I did, but I didn't get anything pertinent out of him. You know, some days his memory seems just fine, and other days I'll ask him a question and he clams up. I'm not sure if he doesn't remember or if he doesn't want to talk about it."

"That doesn't help you find the information you're looking for."

"No, it doesn't." Sarah frowned over Vern's odd lapses of memory.

"I'll get back to you as soon as I find anything."

Sarah went back to her sewing until lunchtime. The phone rang as she walked to the kitchen, and she answered quickly, hoping it was Laura.

"Sarah? It's Martha."

"Well, hi. How are you doing?"

"Feeling a little antsy. But Ernie's having a pretty good day, and it's stopped snowing. What do you say we meet at the café for coffee this afternoon?"

Sarah looked toward the window. Sure enough, the fat, feathery flakes had stopped and only about an inch of new snow had accumulated in the driveway. "I'd love to. It will do us both good to get out. How's two o'clock?"

With the outing planned, she felt more cheerful. She checked her e-mail after she had eaten lunch. A note from Laura strengthened her theory that Vern had dropped out of school to join the army. "Nora Pickett was two grades ahead of Vern," Laura had written. "She went all twelve grades in Concord, graduating in 1940."

In her notebook, Sarah copied the information. Either the family had moved in 1941 or 1942, or Vern's enlistment had cut short his high school career. He wouldn't have been drafted before graduation, but if he'd left school and was eighteen or older, the army would have taken him.

Seventeen if his parents signed for him. But for some reason, this was one topic Vern avoided every time she brought it up.

As Sarah entered The Spotted Dog, she had to walk around a cardboard display unit of romance novels. She gave it a quick glance and smiled. Liam was featuring Vanessa's favorite author.

Martha waved enthusiastically from where she waited at a table.

Sarah unzipped her parka as she walked toward her. "Hi! Am I late?"

"Not at all. Let's get our coffee."

They went to the counter and placed their orders.

"I'm treating today," Sarah said firmly, taking out her debit card.

"Oh—"

"Hush." Sarah handed the card over with a flourish. "I'm paying for both of us."

Karen grinned back. "I hear you, Sarah. Why don't you ladies have a seat, and I'll bring your lattes over in a minute?"

They returned to the quiet seating area and settled in. "How are you doing? Got plenty of meal volunteers?" Sarah asked.

"Pretty well. I need someone to make lunch for Pastor John on Sunday."

"Put me down. I'd be happy to do it."

"But you're doing the food pantry tomorrow."

"It's all right. Really."

"I won't say no." Martha rummaged in her tote bag and came up with a notebook and pen. "Thanks, Sarah. We've discovered there were several other jobs that needed to be done, too, and I think I've called every member of the church at least twice this week. I just remembered last night about the numbers on the hymn board. Angela Miller said she'd change them before she started setting up for her Sunday school class."

"Good. If there's anything else I can do, let me know."

"If I start to go crazy, I'll call you, and you can come calm me down, all right?"

Sarah laughed. "That's a deal. Do you have anyone to pick up the missionary speaker yet?"

"Not yet. Finding someone to do that has become my top priority. I've asked five people so far. Harry Butler's working. His wife is chaperoning her son's skiing trip. The excuses just keep coming." Martha took out her latest crochet project and began to work with her hook as they chatted.

"That's pretty yarn." Sarah leaned closer and eyed the blue ombré. "What are you making?"

"A hat and scarf set for Lexie. I made one for Trina, and now all the granddaughters want one."

Sarah smiled. "That's quite a compliment."

Karen brought over two lattes with lots of whipped cream. "There you go, ladies. Enjoy."

"Thanks, Karen," Sarah said.

"How are you doing on that mystery you were looking into?" Martha asked a moment later.

"I'm progressing by millimeters."

"I guess it could be worse."

"Yes. Anything is better than nothing." Sarah sipped her drink. "This woman, Alice Ward, seems to have dropped off the face of the earth. Even her best friend hasn't heard from her in more than sixty years. Can you believe that?"

Martha frowned as she worked several stitches. "Have you considered that she may be dead?"

"Oh yes. It's very likely, I think. As nearly as I can figure, she'd turn 87 this year if she were alive. Surely she'd have contacted her old friend at some point, when the friend has lived in their hometown all her life."

Martha made a little murmur of sympathy. "Some people don't keep up the old ties."

Sarah took another sip from her cup and gazed across the store as the door opened and admitted Vanessa Sawyer. Sarah waved to her. Liam appeared from the back of the bookstore and hurried toward Vanessa, chatting with her in front of the array of historical romances.

"Looks like Vanessa came to see Liam's display," Sarah said.

Martha turned around to look. "I didn't notice. Is it those medieval books Vanessa likes so much?"

"Yes."

Vanessa detached herself from Liam and walked to their table, smiling broadly.

"Well, hello! I'm taking a quick break—Liam insisted I had to see his new display." She held up a book. "I'm buying the newest one. Can't wait to climb into bed tonight with this."

Martha laughed. "At least those books don't snore."

"So, Sarah, have you started reading the book I lent you?" Vanessa arched her eyebrows.

"Yes, I have. It's quite interesting, though I confess I've only read the first fifty pages or so."

Vanessa's eyes lit. "You're going to love it."

"I was surprised it was set in New England."

"Yes, that was one of her earliest books—maybe the first. It's really good. But I still like the medievals best."

"Maybe she hadn't found her genre yet when she wrote that first one," Martha suggested, counting the stitches in her last row.

"Can you join us for a few minutes?" Sarah asked. "I'll buy you a cup of coffee."

"Thanks, but I really need to run. I don't usually close the store, but no one's been in since noon. I put the 'Back in fifteen' sign on the door, so I need to pay for this book and get going." Vanessa smiled her good-bye and walked over to the cash register.

The next morning, Sarah decided to go to Bradford Manor. She wanted to see Vern briefly and visit her father before going over to the church to help with the monthly opening of the food pantry. The ministry had grown over the past two years, and several families in the community depended on it.

As she drove past the church, she recognized two figures standing nearly knee deep in snow by the sign near the street. Curious, Sarah pulled into the parking lot and rolled down her window.

"Hello! What are you two doing?"

Martha and Ernie turned toward her.

"Hi, Sarah," Martha called. "I realized last night that no one had changed the lettering on the sign for Sunday's service. When I talked to Pastor John, he told me that he usually does it. So Ernie and I decided to come over this morning and put up the name of this week's guest speaker."

"Do you want some help?"

"Oh, we'll be fine."

Ernie grinned and waved. He seemed steady on his feet this morning.

"If you're sure ..."

"Go on," Martha said. "You look like a woman on a mission."

Sarah laughed and put the car in gear. She'd planned to go to Vern's room first, but she met him before she got as far as the hall. He was sitting in the lounge, talking with one of the other residents, Olive Cavanaugh.

Sarah walked over to them. "Hello, Vern. Hello, Olive." She gave a special smile to the elderly woman who had been Jason's Sunday school teacher thirty years earlier.

"Sarah Hart. So nice to see you."

"Thank you. How are you feeling?"

"Just dandy," Olive said.

"Glad to hear it." Sarah turned to Vern. "I'm actually here to see you, as well as my father."

"Have you had any luck finding Bob or . . . " He looked up at her with eyes full of unspoken questions.

"I've learned a few things. Would you like to go down to your room and discuss it?"

They both said good-bye to Olive. Vern rolled his wheelchair down the hall and Sarah followed. When they passed her father's room, she glanced in. William was lying on his bed, and the television set was on.

In his room, Vern turned his wheelchair around. "You said you've found something."

"Yes." Sarah took off her parka and settled in his extra chair. "I'm sorry, Vern, but Bob Willis died a few years ago. I'd hoped I could reunite you with your old friend, but he's gone."

Vern drew in a deep breath and looked down at the carpet. "Well. I'm sorry to hear that. I don't suppose . . . "

"I did find Joan Franklin, though."

He frowned. "Alice's friend?"

Sarah nodded. "I talked with her on the phone. She still lives in Concord, though she's changed her name. She's Mrs. Donald Nash. And she cared deeply about Alice."

"So, is Alice . . . is she alive?"

"I don't know. Neither does Joan. They lost touch a long time ago. I'm thinking of driving over to Concord soon, though I can't do it this weekend." Her commitment at the food pantry would tie her up most of that day, and she didn't want to go on Sunday when she would miss church and the public library would be closed. "The soonest I could do it would be Monday. If I get over there and I find out more, I'll be sure to tell you."

"I appreciate that."

Sarah studied his face for a long moment. "Vern, how are you feeling today?"

"Fine. The therapist said I was doing well." He shrugged. "Guess I'm a little down because of what you told me. I mean, Bob . . ."

"I'm so sorry. I didn't like to bring you that news. Have you thought back to your school days any more?"

"Seems like I've been thinking of nothing else since you took this on."

"Have you remembered any more details? Anything at all that might help me?"

He shook his head. "I don't think so."

"What about your senior year?" she asked gently.

"What about it?"

"You didn't graduate, did you, Vern? You left school. Did you quit so you could join the army?"

Vern sighed. "I suppose maybe I did. It's so long ago now. Those days in the Pacific seem like yesterday, with the enemy popping up out of tunnels in the ground . . . and yet . . . Concord and the family and Alice . . . that's all kind of hazy, you know what I mean?"

"Why didn't you just tell me before that you dropped out of school and enlisted?"

"I don't know. Did you ask?"

"Yes."

"I guess I didn't like talking about it. I mean, not graduating…that's not good. I wish I'd graduated."

"It's nothing to be ashamed of. You served your country well. And since you mentioned family…"

Vern blinked at her but said nothing.

Sarah leaned closer. "Could you tell me about your sister Nora?"

"Nora? What do you want to know?" His eyes flicked away and back to her.

"When did Nora leave Massachusetts? Were she and your parents still there when you went into the army?"

"She…uh…she got married."

"And when was that?"

"Hmm…it was while I was in rehab, I think."

Sarah thought about that while she watched him. "When was that?"

"After Guadalcanal. I was wounded there, you know. When they shipped me stateside, I was in a VA hospital for quite a while."

"I didn't realize how serious your injury was. I'm sorry."

"Well, it wasn't the best time of my life. But I got letters from Nora while they were patching me up. And my mother."

"Your mother was still living then?"

"Yes, she was."

"What about your father?" Sarah gently tried to pry more information from Vern.

Vern shook his head. "He was gone ... he died when I was younger."

"And how long did your mother live?"

"She died ... well ... I think it was '43. She made plans to come by train to visit me at the VA hospital. I told her not to come. It was a long trip, and it would have been hard for her. But she really wanted to see me, so she said she was coming. The next thing I knew, I got a telegram from Nora saying Mother had died. Pneumonia, she said. Quite unexpected."

"Oh, that must have been difficult."

"Well, yes." Vern closed his eyes for a minute.

Had she pushed him enough for one day? His memory of the postbattle period was definitely better than that of his school days.

"So, what did Joan tell you about Alice?" he asked.

"She said that they kept in touch for a few years after school. Joan was expecting company when I called, so we didn't talk too long. But when I suggested that I might visit Concord soon, she invited me to go and see her. If I can get over there, I will. I'm sure she'll share more memories with me." Sarah paused, then said deliberately, "She remembered you."

Vern's eyebrows shot up. "Oh? What did she say?"

"That you'd treated Alice badly."

He looked away.

"That you'd quit writing to her while you were overseas."

"I was wounded."

"Did you tell Alice that?"

He opened his mouth and closed it again.

Sarah said, "Joan didn't think you ever came back after the war. She was surprised to hear you were living in Massachusetts. Alice was devastated when you stopped writing. She probably thought you'd been killed."

"She could have asked Nora or my mother. They'd have told her."

"Maybe she did."

Vern's shoulders drooped.

Definitely enough for this session. Sarah stood. "I'm going to stop in and see my dad. I hope next time I see you I'll have more information about Alice."

Vern looked up at her. "When you said you'd talked to Joan, I hoped she'd told you where to find Alice. Do you really think there's still a chance of finding her?"

The pain in his voice was so strong, Sarah couldn't help but forgive him his youthful thoughtlessness. "I don't know, but I'll keep searching."

After a brief visit with her father, she went out to her car and drove down the hill into town. She pulled into the church parking lot. To her surprise, Martha and Ernie were still out there, down on their hands and knees in the snow.

 CHAPTER NINE

Sarah nosed her Grand Prix into a parking space and jumped out.

"What happened? Why are you still here?"

Martha reached out to steady herself on one of the legs of the signboard and stood slowly. Clumps of snow clung to the knees of her dark slacks.

"Oh, Sarah, I dropped the box of letters. Guess I should have taken out the ones we needed when we found it in the pastor's office, but I wasn't thinking. We were doing fine until I missed my footing on the step stool, and splat! They went everywhere. Ernie and I have been digging Xs and Rs out of the snow for the last twenty minutes."

"We'd be done with the sign, except we can't find another P," Ernie said.

Martha looked close to tears. "I know there's another one somewhere. There has to be. But we've churned up the snow so much, I can't tell where we've looked and where we haven't."

"Would it be so horrible if you were missing one letter P?" Sarah asked.

"You tell me." Martha jerked her chin toward the sign.

Sarah read the sign carefully. Aloud she said, "Guest minister Rev. Edward—"

"Spinner," said Ernie. "His last name is *supposed* to be Spinner."

"Oh. *Oh!*" Sarah laughed. "I see what you mean. Come on, I'll help you look. Isn't there a shovel in the closet just inside the front door? And if we can't find it, maybe it would be better to borrow the P from 'worship.'"

"That's the sanest thing I've heard all morning." Martha turned toward the church. "I'll go look for the shovel. I think I've bent over enough for today."

Sarah turned up two Bs, an A, and a T with the shovel before she finally recovered the missing P. Ernie climbed the step stool and placed it in the visiting minister's name. Sarah noted that his hands shook a little as he fitted it into the sign. She stood close to the stool, waiting anxiously until he was safely on the ground again. He must be exhausted, but he hadn't complained or blamed Martha for the mishap. Seeing the two of them still working together contentedly after all their years of marriage sent a sudden pang through Sarah's heart, and she thought of Gerry and all the moments they'd shared one task or another.

She smiled up at Ernie. "Remember the year the church had the live nativity out front at Christmas time? You and Gerry built the stable together."

Ernie laughed. "Yeah, and it dumped a foot of snow the night before. We kept losing our tools then too. I don't think Jerry found his staple gun until spring."

"But that was so much fun," Martha said. "Everyone in town came to see it. And the goat got loose and we all had to chase it." She laughed. "Maybe we should think about doing it again next year, but let the young people tend the animals."

Sarah smiled at her friends. "That sounds like a great idea. All right, you two, that's a good job done. I'll put the shovel and the box of letters away. I wish I could go home with you and make us all a pot of tea, but it's nearly time to open the food pantry." Two more cars had entered the parking lot, and she knew Harry and Belle were probably waiting for her inside.

"Thank you, Sarah." Martha seemed only too glad to lead Ernie to their car, where she took the driver's seat.

Sarah quickly returned the box and the shovel to their places in the church and hurried downstairs. Harry and Belle had set up in the fellowship hall, and several patrons of the food pantry had already arrived.

"Hi, Sarah," Belle called. "We were afraid you'd forgotten."

"No, I had an unexpected task I had to do. Sorry about that." She put on the apron Belle handed her.

"Ready?" Harry Butler asked, setting a case of canned vegetables on the counter.

"Ready." As Sarah helped people choose the items they needed, she reflected that Pastor John would certainly be appreciated when he was able to resume his duties— although she'd begun to think he shouldn't have to resume them all. John Peabody dealt with far more tasks than she or anyone else in the church had realized. And she was starting to think Martha was putting in too much time making sure all the jobs were done in the meantime.

Sunday dawned bright and sunny. Sarah got up early and filled her bird feeder. She loved to watch the chickadees and cedar waxwings flutter around for the seeds. Next she put together a meal basket for Pastor John. She tucked a chocolate bar and a book of crossword puzzles Belle had donated into the basket.

She enjoyed the worship service, but she couldn't help smiling when Harry Butler introduced the Reverend Spinner, remembering the sign crisis. She glanced over at Martha. Her friend was shaking, red-faced from holding back a laugh. Sarah looked straight ahead and breathed slowly and deeply until the almost overwhelming urge to giggle left her.

After the service, Maggie made her way across the aisle to Sarah. "You're coming over for lunch, aren't you, Sarah?"

"Yes, I'll be there in a few minutes. I made dinner for Pastor John, and I'm going to take it over now, along with a tape of the service."

Sarah went to the recording station, where Martha caught her.

"Sarah, you're taking lunch to Pastor John today, right?"

"Yes, I'm on my way there now."

"Thank you. I'm trying to line up volunteers for the rest of the week, but it's getting harder. People have a lot of excuses, and when I started calling them the second time around, a lot of women put me off. Some don't want to drive in the snow, but some just don't want to bother to cook. One family's got out-of-town company. Another woman said she didn't feel confident cooking for the pastor. I told her that it doesn't have to be fancy, but I don't think I convinced her."

"I'm sorry."

Martha sighed. "Pastor John feels like he's putting people out, and I guess some of the cooks in this church feel that way too. But Harry is going over this evening, and he offered to pick up some takeout food for both of them for supper."

"Is Harry staying overnight?"

"No, John says he's all right on his own now." Martha's forehead furrowed. "I worry about him being alone. It's been only ten days since his accident. But there don't seem to be any men who can sleep over there. Ernie offered, but if he went over there, I'd worry about both of them."

"Is Pastor John up on crutches?"

"He's still supposed to be using the wheelchair, but he has a doctor's appointment tomorrow. If everything's mending well, he'll be able to use the crutches, and soon he'll be fending for himself again."

"Would you like me to help you make some of the calls to line up meals?" Sarah asked.

"Thanks, but I know you're headed to Concord tomorrow. I think we're set through Tuesday, and I can take lunch over Wednesday if no one else will."

The tape was ready, and Sarah hurried out to her car. The pastor's house was only a short way down the street, but she drove over. When she rang the doorbell, she thought she heard a response from inside, but with cars driving past, it was hard to tell. She opened the door and stepped in, calling, "Your dinner is here, Pastor John. It's me, Sarah."

"Sarah? I'm in the living room!"

The reverend's voice sounded a little weak. Perhaps she'd woken him from a nap. Sarah stepped inside, carrying her basket, and closed the door firmly behind her.

"Hello, Pastor—" She gasped as she spotted his tall, lean form lying on the carpet near the recliner. The wheelchair stood a couple of feet away from him. "John! Are you all right?" She ran across the room and knelt beside him, setting the basket down on the floor.

"I've been better." He reached out and clutched her hand. "Sarah, I'm so glad you came. I was sure someone would be along soon, so I've tried to be patient, but I have to admit I haven't been totally successful." His smile morphed into a grimace.

"You've hurt your ankle again."

"I'm afraid so. Trying to pick myself up didn't help, either."

"How long have you been on the floor?" she asked.

"Not more than thirty minutes. I prayed that Reverend Spinner wouldn't preach overtime. Imagine that."

Sarah tried to smile, but her concern for the pastor's health won out over her sense of humor. "Didn't you have your cell phone?"

"I'm afraid it fell out of my pocket in the chair. I'm still kicking myself for that—or I would be if I were able. I'm getting so tired of being helpless!"

"Do you think you'll be all right if I get some help to lift you, or should you go to the emergency room?"

"I don't think I've added more than a few new bruises. I admit, I tried to get up by myself, and I shouldn't have. I had far too much confidence in my own ability. And once I was down, I couldn't get up. Ah, Sarah, what would I do if you didn't come to my rescue every time I needed it?"

"I'm sure the Lord would send someone else. Hold on, and we'll put you back to rights." Sarah rose and took out her own phone.

Jason answered on the second ring.

"Jason, where are you? Are you still at church?"

"We're just about to leave, Mom. What's up?"

"I'm at Pastor John's, and he's fallen. Can you come over and help me get him back into his chair?"

"Sure, I'll be right there. Should I grab one of the other men?"

"That might be best."

Jason and Maggie arrived a minute later, with Harry Butler close behind. They hurried into the living room.

"John, are you all right?" Harry asked as he entered.

"Ah, Harry. We've got to stop meeting like this."

Harry chuckled. "I'm glad you're not past the laughing stage. We'll get you up. Do you want to get into the chair, or would you rather go to bed for a while?"

"I think perhaps I'm due for a nap. After my noon medication, that is."

"Oh, I almost forgot," Sarah said. "I brought lunch. If I heated your plate in the microwave, would you feel up to eating some chicken pie?"

"I think I might," Pastor John said, "but ask me again when I'm propped up in bed, will you?"

Sarah and Maggie went to the kitchen and prepared a tray. By the time the pastor's plate had warmed, Jason came in.

"He's in his bed, leaning against a mound of pillows. Better let me take his lunch in—Harry and I helped him undress."

"Oh, dear. Do you think he should see the doctor now?"

Jason shrugged. "He says not. He's going tomorrow anyway, and he doesn't think he did any serious damage today. He's got quite a bruise on his cheek, though. Mostly, he's feeling helpless right now."

Jason carried the tray to the bedroom, and Harry took his leave.

"Oh, we need to find his cell phone," Sarah said. "If he hadn't dropped it, he could have called for help sooner."

She and Maggie searched in and under the recliner.

"Here it is." Maggie pulled the phone from between the cushions and went to hand it to Jason to give to the pastor.

A few minutes later, Jason came back to the kitchen. "All set, ladies. Shall we proceed to lunch?"

After their dinner, the twins cleared the table, and Sarah volunteered to help Maggie load the dishwasher.

"I can't believe all you've done to this house," Sarah said as they worked. Jason and Maggie had snapped up the chance to buy the old house that had once belonged to Sarah's grandfather and had begun the process of restoring it. Sarah especially loved Maggie's kitchen, with its granite countertop, vintage cabinets, pine floor, and persimmon-colored walls.

"Well, we've slowed down this winter, but yeah, we have accomplished a lot." Maggie smiled. "I really love this house. Some days I regret not getting to spend more time here."

Sarah smiled, knowing how Maggie struggled to balance her business with her family time. "I'm driving over to Concord tomorrow."

"Oh? What for?" Maggie asked.

"You know I'm looking for an old friend of one of the residents at Bradford Manor? Well, I haven't found his high school sweetheart yet, but I have located her best friend Joan. And Joan still lives in their hometown, which is

Concord. She invited me to have lunch with her tomorrow. I'm driving over to meet her and do some research at their library."

"It won't be too bad a drive if the weather cooperates," Maggie said.

"That's what I think."

"Just drive safely."

Sarah got a clean dishcloth from a drawer and turned on the hot water faucet.

"Here, I'll wipe up," Maggie said. "You go in and talk to the girls for a few minutes. Then I need to shoo them upstairs to do their homework."

Sarah handed her the wet cloth.

The telephone rang, and Maggie answered it. "Well, hi! Yes, she is. Just a minute." She put her hand over the receiver, smiling. "It's your daughter."

"Oh, thank you!" Sarah took the phone. "Jenna?"

"Hi, Mom. I tried your house and you weren't there, so I thought I might find you here."

"I'm so glad you did! How are you all doing?"

She and Jenna had a good chat, and after a few minutes Sarah told her about her plans to go to Concord and her purpose there.

"Oh, Mom, you and your mysteries. Sometimes I worry about you."

"No need for that," Sarah assured her. "This one is very tame. I'm only going to visit the library and have lunch with an elderly lady."

"I wonder what Dad would say if he were there now?" Jenna mused.

"He'd probably say, 'All right, but I'm driving. When do we leave?'"

Jenna's laugh buoyed Sarah. "You may be right. Dad was usually game for anything you wanted to do. I know he'd be proud of the things you've accomplished lately."

Sarah felt tears welling in her eyes. Gerry would think this sleuthing business was grand fun. "Thank you, honey. Pray that I'll be able to find the woman I'm looking for. It means a lot to my new friend Vern."

 **CHAPTER TEN**

Sarah set out for Concord early Monday morning, anticipating her meeting with Joan and touching base with Laura Baird at the library. She arrived in town just after ten and went straight to the library. The graceful Georgian building seemed like the ideal place to work. She went inside and unzipped her jacket, looking around. At the circulation desk, she asked for Laura.

"Mrs. Hart!" Laura came from a small office, smiling and extending her hand.

"Please call me Sarah. It's so good to meet you."

"Thank you. How can I help you today?"

"I'm having lunch with Joan Nash, and I suspect that I may want to come back here with a long list of questions after I've talked to her."

"Wonderful. I work until four today."

"Perfect. Is it possible for me to see those Concord High School yearbooks you consulted for me?"

"Of course."

Laura went for the school annuals while Sarah settled in at a reading table and took out her glasses.

"Here's the annual for the class of 1942." Laura laid several padded volumes on the table and opened the top one. She flipped to the senior section. "Here's Joan Franklin."

The young Joan wasn't nearly as pretty as Alice, but she had an air of mischief and fun about her that some boys must have found very attractive.

"I like that picture."

"Yes, she was cute." Laura turned several pages. "Here's Alice."

Sarah nodded. "The photo Vern lent me is a copy of that one. It's rather worn. He said he carried it to the Pacific and back with him."

"How romantic." Laura pointed. "Across the page here is Bob Willis's picture."

The young man's grave demeanor made him look older than some of the other students. Sarah wondered if his mind was already on the military. She read the lists of extracurricular activities beneath the picture again. "I wonder what drew him and Vern together."

"Hard to say. As I told you, there's no picture of Vern in the yearbook. I looked through it carefully, hoping to find a candid, but if he's in here, his photo wasn't labeled."

"What about previous years?" Sarah asked.

Laura opened another book. "There's a tiny head shot in this one, his junior year, but it's not very good."

Sarah took the volume and squinted at the photo Laura indicated. The small picture didn't do the young man justice. She shook her head. "I saw a picture of him in his uniform. Of course, he was a bit older then." She wished she could see the photo enlarged.

She leafed through the 1942 yearbook again. In the back were several pages of display ads. She smiled as she read the names of the businesses. She remembered when she was in high school, helping her class canvass merchants and professionals in Maple Hill to sponsor the yearbook.

A one-eighth page ad on the lower left caught her eye. Sarah caught her breath. "Ward and Tindell, Attorneys-at-Law. Do you think that could be Alice's father's firm?"

Laura looked. "It might very well be. Alice's father would probably contribute to the cause and take out an ad."

"But he died that year," Sarah said, unsure how this discovery would help. "Do you recognize this Tindell name?"

Laura frowned. "There's a law office on Walden Street with that name. Let me grab the phone book."

Laura came back with a telephone directory in her hand. "Tindell, Tindell & Harmon. Here's their number."

"Thank you so much."

Laura gave her a nod. "If I can help you in any way, just come find me."

A secretary answered Sarah's call, and Sarah tried to keep her voice down as she gave her name.

"I'm searching for information about a family named Ward that used to live in Concord. Mr. Ward was an attorney, and his partner was named Tindell."

"Robert Ward," the secretary said at once. "He died back in the fifties, I think, or even before that. Mr. Tindell took over the practice after his death. The elder Mr. Tindell, that is."

Sarah felt as though her smile might split her face. "In that case, I'd like to make an appointment to speak to him. This afternoon, if possible."

Sarah drove to Joan's house, arriving just before noon. With a mantle of snow on its roof, the white clapboard house held a grace and charm. The solid square corner pilasters, central chimney, and broad lintel over the door gave away the age of the house.

Joan opened the door to Sarah with an energetic sweep. Though her hair was as white as cotton balls, there was nothing else fluffy about this woman. Joan wore a smart cropped gray jacket and woolen pants, with a rose-colored blouse. Her blue eyes sparkled, and she stood upright as though defying her age.

"Sarah Hart. Come in. I'm delighted to have you here." Joan stepped back to allow Sarah entry.

Sarah walked into a sunny room full of color and pleasing textures—baskets, antique crockery, pewter candlesticks, and overstuffed cushions that welcomed her as if she were an old friend.

"How lovely," she murmured as she handed Joan her coat.

"Thank you. Sit down, please." Joan took a seat in a rocker next to the bay window, and Sarah sat on a settee nearby.

"I'm happy to have the chance to consult an expert on the town of Concord," Sarah said. "I know there's so much local history that I think my granddaughters will find interesting. I plan to bring them here next summer."

"They'd probably like to walk up to Author's Ridge in the cemetery. And did you know the mounted police have a stable out by Walden Pond? Girls love that."

Sarah pulled out her notebook and scribbled a few notes about places to make sure she visited with the twins. "Thank you. But I suppose I should tell you a little more about why I came by today. I need to make some progress on Vern's puzzle if I can."

"I hope I can be of some help to you, though I'm not sure how," Joan said. "Shall we discuss it over lunch?"

She led Sarah to the dining area, which opened from her low-beamed kitchen. Since Joan walked slowly, Sarah had time to absorb each new treasure that met her gaze—a display of half a dozen butter molds on a low piecrust table especially caught her eye. A paperback copy of Hawthorne's *The Blithedale Romance* lay next to them, with a bookmark protruding from the pages.

When they had begun to eat, Joan said, "How did you meet Vern?"

"He's in a nursing home for rehabilitation from a fall. My father is in the same place." Sarah paused. "I get the feeling Vern has things he'd like to tell Alice that he's put off for decades. It will be very sad if he never gets the chance to say those things."

"I see. But Vern—his mind is still good?"

"Oh yes, for the most part. His memory seems a bit vague when it comes to prewar events. Before 1942, that is."

"That's too bad. Those were good years—at least for me they were. I look back on high school as a bittersweet time. We were so innocent, not knowing what lay ahead."

"I've learned that Vern didn't graduate with his class," Sarah ventured.

"That's right. He dropped out our senior year. Such a shame. He ought to have waited until after graduation. Do you know what he did for a living after the war?"

"I don't know what he did immediately after, but he'd been the manager of a hardware store for some time before he retired."

"Hmm. He used to say he wanted to be a writer."

Sarah tried to reconcile that with the elderly man she knew. "Did he do well in school?"

"Yes, I think so. We weren't close, you understand, but Alice talked about him a lot. She thought he was the next poetic genius."

"A poet?" Sarah frowned. "In the short time I've known Vern, I'd have said he was very prosaic."

"Oh, how we change. What I don't understand is how he can have the nerve to look for Alice now, after what he did to her back then."

Sarah eyed her cautiously. "Could you be more specific, please?"

"He broke her heart, that's all. Led her on, then all of a sudden left. He wrote to her at first. For quite a while, actually. She planned on marrying him when he came back. I know she did. And then, poof! He was gone for good. No more letters. Nothing."

Sarah took a deep breath. She was sure that if Vern had been in the room, Joan would have given him a good shaking, and Sarah felt a bit put out with him herself.

Joan paused with her fork in midair. "I don't suppose he's told you why he stopped writing to her so suddenly?"

"No. Only that he was wounded and laid up for a long time."

Joan pursed her lips for a moment. "I did hear that he was wounded. I suppose he might have had a lot of dark thoughts then—on how he might not be the same man. He wasn't permanently disabled, though, was he?"

"No, he wasn't."

"Well, it seems to me there's as much of a mystery on Vern's side of this as there is on Alice's."

"Do you have any pictures of Vern?" Sarah asked.

"I don't think so. I looked through my old albums after we talked on the phone. Of course, he didn't hang around with our usual set. I think he had to work after school most days. His family didn't have much money."

When they'd finished their lunch, Joan brought a pot of tea and a plate of fruit tarts to the living room, and they sat down together. She showed Sarah some of her pictures from her high school years. One was of two girls sitting on the grass, waving.

"That's Alice and me. We had some great times together. Especially after she got her car."

"Oh yes, the 1939 Chevy. Vern certainly remembers that car clearly."

"It made a big difference in his life, I guess—being noticed by the only girl in school who had her own car." Joan sighed. "Poor Alice. I wish I knew what happened to her."

"Tell me what you do know." Sarah closed the album and took out her notebook.

Joan settled back against the cushions cradling her mug of tea. "Concord is a wonderful town to grow up in. My father had the grocery back in the '30s and '40s. Money was always a little tight, but not so tight it hurt. Alice's father was a lawyer—quite a prominent attorney in this area. He had an office here, but he was always going into Boston for court cases."

Sarah nodded. "I'm going to the law office later and speak to his old partner's son."

"Are you? Maybe they can tell you something about the family."

"Would you say that Alice was considered part of the town's upper class?"

"You might say that. But she was a sweet, genuine girl."

"I'm almost surprised she didn't go to the private academy instead of the public high school."

"That was her choice. Her father did lean toward putting her in the academy, but she wanted to stay with her friends. She and I were classmates from first grade on. She knew her family had more money than most of ours did, but she didn't let that keep her from making friends. She was never a snob. I guess Vern is proof of that."

"She fell for a boy from the lower class."

"Yes. And back then, it mattered. To her folks, I mean. Especially to her folks. Status was very important to them." Joan smiled. "I think that car was about status, so far as her father was concerned. Not many of the kids had cars back then. A few of the boys had beat-up old jalopies, but Mr. Ward wanted Alice to have something nicer. Something befitting her position, you know. Not a brand-new car. That would be too expensive and too ostentatious, even for him. Oh, *he* would drive a brand-new car and trade it every second year. But not his daughter, while she was still in high school. Still, just having a car at all placed Alice in a bracket above the rest of the students—she'd just finished her junior year when she got it."

"The car was a reward for her grades, wasn't it?" Sarah asked.

"Yes. She turned seventeen that summer, and Mr. Ward said the car was partly her birthday present and partly in honor of her excellent report card. It was blue, and the seat covers were dark blue leather." Joan let out a deep sigh. "Alice loved that car."

"And you got to ride in it."

"Oh, yes. All the time. She'd take a few other girlfriends sometimes, too, but I was her regular chum and her steady rider. Back and forth to school that fall, and to Casey's drugstore. That was where we'd go for sodas sometimes. I couldn't afford to go every day, but Alice treated me a lot. We probably went a couple of times a week."

"Your parents weren't worried about you riding around in the car with her?"

"Oddly enough, as I look back at it, no. They trusted me, and they considered Alice to be a levelheaded, responsible girl. And for the most part, she was."

"For the most part?" Sarah arched her eyebrows.

"Well, there was Vern, you know."

"Ah, of course. Alice's one irresponsible move."

"Yes. It was a daring adventure for her, flirting with Vern, and later on meeting him on the sly. She was crazy about him that year."

"What was the attraction?"

"Oh, I don't know. Partly the 'bad boy' aspect, though Vern wasn't really bad. I don't know that he'd had any trouble with the law. But he was poor and a little tough. His father was gone. Whether he'd died or abandoned the family, I'm not sure. And Vern was very good looking." She smiled. "Eyes like Paul Newman. But not the sort of fellow Alice's daddy would have chosen for her."

"Yes, I can imagine that. So, her father didn't like Vern. Or didn't he know about him?"

"He knew. He forbade Alice to see him."

Sarah caught her breath. "I had no idea."

Joan nodded, her mouth set in a grim line. "Her father could be very obstinate. Alice could be too, but she didn't express it openly. She started seeing Vern secretly. Even though she knew it was wrong, she enjoyed it tremendously."

"Forbidden fruit," Sarah murmured.

"And Vern was a charming boy. Not my type, but I could understand why she liked him." Joan hesitated, then smiled at Sarah with a confessional air. "Sometimes I acted as their go-between. I'd take notes back and forth between them, and a couple of times I called the Wards' house and invited Alice over as a ruse so she could go and meet Vern without her parents knowing. It seemed very romantic."

"That must have been thrilling."

"It was, in a way. I'd never had a steady boyfriend up to that point, and of course I wanted to help Alice find happiness and true love. She was sure that she and Vern were made for each other, and so I believed it. Now I can see that she needed a strong, steady man, not a flighty lad with a hot temper."

"Vern had a temper?" Sarah sipped her tea.

"Well, yes. But he had nothing over her father on that score. When Mr. Ward found out Alice had been seeing Vern after he'd told her not to, he was furious."

"When was that?"

"I think it was right before Thanksgiving. Yes, it was senior year just at the holiday break. Vern dropped out of school. Alice was distraught. She stopped by the gas station, and the boss told her Vern hadn't been to work over the weekend. He was fuming about it. Alice hunted his sister up after school the next week, to ask where he was. I went with her, and Nora told us that Vern had joined the service. Alice was shattered that he'd gone without seeing her first."

"I expect that would leave a seventeen-year-old girl heartbroken."

"It did. Alice was worried sick. I was afraid she'd do something foolish. Fight with her father, or ... or something worse. But she went all quiet and martyrlike. I didn't know how to act around her for the next week or so. And then ..."

"Then?" Sarah asked.

"Pearl Harbor. It changed everything. Oh, and Alice's father died suddenly, too. It was a very rough year for Alice."

"I should say so." Sarah made more notes. "What happened in the spring? You both graduated."

"Yes. Alice was still grieving over her father, and over Vern's sudden departure, though she'd had a few letters from him by then. That's what got her through that ghastly summer. Vern wrote to her from outlandish places, and the letters didn't really say much. But she treasured them. Meanwhile, I had to work in my father's store that summer, to earn money for college. But Alice's father had provided for her schooling, so she stayed close to home with her mother. I didn't see much of her that summer. We both went to Radcliffe in September, and we got to room together. We'd drive Alice's car home on weekends. That freshman year, I was still close to Alice—in some ways closer than ever before."

"So what happened?" Sarah asked. "How did you drift apart?"

"It was very sad. Sometime after Christmas, the letters from Vern stopped coming. They just...stopped. Alice was depressed for a long time. She was certain he'd been killed. But then Vern's mother put it about that she'd heard from him. That stung. He was writing to his mother, but not to Alice. Then we heard he'd been shot and was in a hospital somewhere. Virginia, maybe? She went to see Mrs. Pickett once. I don't know what passed between them, but I do know Alice never got any more letters from Vern."

"Did she stay at Radcliffe?"

"Yes. She went through sophomore year all silent and determined to be at the top of her class. So sober and unlike herself, she was then. I started dating Donald that year, but Alice was at a low point. And when Vern's mother died, she went into an even deeper depression."

"Why was that?" Sarah asked.

"I think it was because his family was all gone then. There were no ties to bring Vern back to Concord anymore. Nora had moved out West, and came back to take care of her mother's things. I'm not sure if Alice saw her or not. It was all very sad." Joan sat for a moment reflecting on the past, then brightened. "But what do you know? Our third year, she met someone."

"Aha. Tell me about him."

"He was a student—studying engineering. And he cracked through her shell somehow. Russell Farmer was his name. Alice and I graduated in 1946, and Donald and I were married a week later. Alice stayed with her mother that summer, but she'd accepted Russell's proposal. They got married in August. I was her bridesmaid. She and Russell left town at once for his new job. I missed her terribly."

"So they left the area right away?"

"Russell got a job out West, and Alice went with him right after the wedding. I wrote to her at least once a week, and she wrote back. She seemed happy." Joan shook her head. "The last address I have for her was in Colorado. Russell had a job connected to the mines out there. I can get the address for you, if you think it will do any good, but my last few letters came back unopened."

"Yes, I'd like to have the address, if it's not too much trouble." Sarah waited while Joan got it. As she copied it into her notebook, Sarah said, "You and Alice remained good friends after she married. Do you have any idea what made her stop writing?"

"Not a clue. I wondered at the time if she'd died. But wouldn't you think Russell would have had the decency to tell me? And they had a little daughter."

Sarah caught her breath. "A little girl?"

"Yes. I never saw the baby, but Alice sent a couple of pictures. She was an adorable child. But then I never heard from her again."

"Do you think they could have moved?" Sarah asked.

"Yes, at least after awhile. I sent several letters and tried to telephone, but I got no response. My last two letters came back with no forwarding address."

Sarah couldn't help thinking that Alice had treated Joan the same way Vern had treated her. "But Alice's mother— didn't she still live here?"

"She'd moved away as well by that time. I thought perhaps she'd gone out to be with Alice. I've always wondered what became of my dearest friend." Joan dabbed at her eyes with a tissue and blinked at Sarah. "Wouldn't you think that after awhile she'd send me a card or something, just to let me know she was all right?"

Sarah reached over and patted her hand. "One would think so. I'm sorry, Joan."

"Yes." Joan gave a big sigh. "We were like sisters then. All these years I've thought she must be dead."

CHAPTER ELEVEN

An hour later, Sarah arrived at the law office, located in an old, two-story house. As she entered, the detailed woodwork and period wallpaper made her feel welcome. She paused to admire a hand-quilted wall hanging in the waiting area. A few minutes later, a well-groomed office assistant ushered her into Jeremy Tindell's private office.

"Thank you so much for seeing me." She extended her hand to him.

"You're welcome. I haven't much time, but I admit you've piqued my curiosity. Please have a seat."

Sarah sat in a leather armchair and settled back to assess him in comfort. Tindell was younger than she—fifty, perhaps, with sleek dark hair and wings of gray at his temples. He had a slim build, and his tailored suit added to his air of distinction.

"I want to find out all I can about Alice Ward and her family," she said.

Tindell nodded. "I never knew Alice. She was gone before I was born. My grandfather was the partner here at the time you mentioned—in practice with Robert Ward. In fact, Mr. Ward was the senior partner. But when he died, my grandfather took over the practice. He bought out the widow—Mrs. Lavinia Ward, who was Alice's mother."

"I see. Do you happen to know what happened to Lavinia and Alice after Mr. Ward died? Especially Alice. I know she got married a few years later and moved to Colorado. From there, I haven't been able to pick up the trail."

"By that time, the sale of the business was long over," Tindell said. "I don't really know what became of the family. I'm sorry." He glanced at his watch. "I could show you a picture of Mr. Ward. His portrait is still hanging in our conference room, as founder of the firm."

"I'd love to see it."

He led her out through the lobby. As they passed through, the receptionist looked up. Tindell paused.

"Arlene, would you please look up any information we have about Robert Ward's death and my grandfather's purchase of his share of the firm?"

"Yes, sir."

"Thank you," he said. "We'll be in the conference room."

Sarah followed him into the room, which held a long, polished table and seating for eight. On one wall hung a ship model in a glass case, and across from it were two portraits in heavy gold frames. Tindell paused at the nearer one.

"This is Mr. Ward. My grandfather's over there." He nodded toward the other picture.

Sarah gazed up at the portrait. She had expected a thin, hawk-nosed man with a disapproving expression. Instead she saw a plump man with thinning hair and a large mustache. His face, while not jolly, wasn't nearly as severe as she had thought it would be. A man who loved his daughter, Sarah surmised, and wanted only the best for her.

"Was Alice an only child, do you know?"

"I believe so." Tindell paused. "Yes, I'm almost certain."

When they went back to the lobby, a man and a woman were seated in chairs, and they looked up with interest as Sarah and Tindell entered. The receptionist rose from her chair.

"I found the file you wanted, Mr. Tindell." She handed him a folder.

He opened it and flipped through a few pages. "Yes, it's just as I thought. Grandpa bought the Ward interest in the firm within a month after Mr. Ward's death. He gave Mrs. Ward a fair price."

"Does it give her address?" Sarah asked.

"Yes. She was still living here in town at that time."

"And there's nothing further, telling where she moved to later?"

"I'm afraid not."

Sarah was disappointed, but she tried not to let it show. "Thank you very much. Even though you didn't know Alice

Ward or her father personally, you've helped me get to know them better."

"There's a program from Mr. Ward's funeral. Would you like a copy?"

"Yes, please."

The receptionist took it and copied it for her.

Tindell put the original back in the folder and closed it. "It sounds as if you have your work cut out for you. I wish you success."

On Tuesday morning, Sarah baked muffins and then took half a dozen to Pastor John. It wasn't her turn to take a meal, but she wanted to see firsthand how he had recovered from his second fall.

"Come right in," he called when she knocked.

Sarah stepped inside and poked her head in at the living room doorway. The pastor sat in the wheelchair opposite the recliner.

"Well, this is a change."

"Yes. I decided I could do quite a lot for myself if I could wheel about this room, the kitchen, and the downstairs bedroom that I've been using these past couple of weeks. I'm extremely careful, and so far so good."

"Take your time," Sarah said. "It must be difficult to get into and out of that wheelchair alone without putting weight on your ankle. You just take it easy until the doctor says you're ready."

"Well, the doctor says I can use my crutches a little if I'm careful, but it's still painful, so he said to use the chair when I can for another week or two."

"In that case, I'm glad you're following his advice." She held out the bag of muffins. "Are you hungry?"

"Those look delicious."

"I hope you like them. I had one this morning and they're not too bad. Would you like me to heat one up for you?"

"Won't you join me?"

"Perhaps just for a cup of tea. I've had plenty of muffins already this morning."

When Sarah returned with their refreshments, she sat down with him. "Now, tell me exactly what the doctor said yesterday."

"He said it's coming along nicely, but 'at my age' I should be cautious." Pastor John glared, then grinned. "His words, not mine. Seems mature people like us don't heal as quickly as youngsters."

"Did he think your fall on Sunday did any further damage?"

"No, but I have a lovely purple bruise on my *other* leg now. Tell me what you've been up to lately."

Sarah unwound her latest mystery for him, beginning with the first time she met Vern. Pastor John followed her narrative with interest.

"So, after he recovered from his wound, did he go back to join his unit?" Pastor John asked.

"You know, I didn't think to ask him that. He was wounded at Guadalcanal, so that means February of 1943 at the latest, according to my research. I wonder where the rest of the Americal Division was while he was recuperating. His mother died while he was hospitalized, and I'm pretty sure he didn't go home afterward." She smiled at him. "Thanks. I'll do some more reading about his division. It would be good to know if he went back to the war or was discharged from the army."

After they finished their tea, Sarah left Pastor John and went on to Maggie's store. Maggie was with customers, so Sarah browsed, noticing that her daughter-in-law had added some new merchandise since her last visit.

"I'm so glad you came," Maggie cried when the customers had left the store.

Sarah met her in the aisle for a hug. "I just stopped in to say hello. Looks like the snow didn't deter customers for too long!"

"So far, business has been worthwhile. If we don't get many more snow days, I should be all right. Look at what I found." Maggie steered her into the kitchen section.

Sarah's gaze fell on a half dozen finely embroidered dish towels with crocheted edgings. "Oh, beautiful!"

Maggie held one up. "Antique linens are all the rage now—kitchen towels, dresser scarves, doilies. I've had several customers ask me if I had any. I got these in an online auction, and I'm very pleased with the quality."

"We'll have to watch for some at yard sales this summer." Sarah fingered the fine satin-stitch flowers on one of the dish towels. "This is painstaking work for an everyday item."

"Yes. I had two with tatted edgings, and a customer snapped them up the day after I put them on display. Women did beautiful work back then—before computers and television and all the other distractions we have now."

The bell on the door rang as another customer entered. "I hear we may get more snow," Maggie said as they walked toward the front of the shop.

Sarah shook her head. "I wouldn't worry too much about it. I had the radio on while I drove over here, and it sounds like it's not going to amount to much."

After a quick stop at the post office to mail a package to Jenna, Sarah drove home and put in a solid two hours on her latest column for *Country Cottage,* the magazine she had recently begun to contribute to, then took up her quilting project. She was ready to add the borders to Vern's quilt, and she set about it with all the information she had gathered brewing in her mind.

That evening, after supper with Belle, she was too tired to continue sewing. Instead, she picked up the novel Vanessa had lent her and sat down in her rocker.

She was more than a third of the way through the book, and she had come to a critical point. The young heroine, Ellie, lived in a small New England town. She was popular in school and oblivious to the impending war though the people around her talked about it incessantly. It was 1940, and they had come out of the Depression. Money wasn't as tight as it had been. She had plenty of stylish new clothes for school in the fall. She and her girlfriends studied together, talked about boys, and went to the drugstore after school for a soda or a hamburger. At the drugstore, Ellie met Riley, a boy with a bad reputation. Sarah smiled when she read that, thinking of Alice. The plot wasn't unique, but the author told it with flair and passion.

Sarah read on. Ellie started sneaking out to see Riley. She avoided lying directly to her parents, but she let them think things that weren't true to cover up her activities. And Riley pressured her to give up the staid and predictable life her parents were grooming her for. Ellie stood on the brink of womanhood, believing she was ready to take the plunge.

Then Ellie's father bought her a car. A blue 1939 Chevrolet.

Stunned, Sarah laid down the book and stared at the dying fire in the fireplace, finding it hard to think straight. Could this be some sort of practical joke? This detail was identical to what Vern had told her and Joan Nash had confirmed about Alice Ward's car. The plot about a well-to-do girl falling for a poor boy her parents disliked could probably be found in many romance novels, but the car had brought Sarah to a screeching halt. She thought back over the way she'd met Vern at the nursing home and her early investigation into the Ward family and Alice's classmates.

Vanessa had lent her the book weeks before that. The coincidence seemed too great to ignore.

She got up and went to her sewing room. Online, she did a search on the author's name: Marjory Middlefield. The name brought up hundreds of hits, but most of them were offers of the author's books for sale. Didn't she have a Web site? Every author had one—or so Sarah had believed.

Every path she followed on her computer led to a dead end. She went to the site of a large bookseller and searched for an author page. The retailer had set up a page displaying all of Middlefield's book covers and offering copies for sale, but it didn't include a photo of the author, an interview, or even a brief biographical note.

Discouraged, Sarah punched in the author's name at an online encyclopedia site. It brought up a short article consisting mainly of a list of Middlefield's books. The book Sarah was reading—*Before the Storm*—was the earliest, published in 1952. Sarah sat back and stared at the screen. She'd heard of authors and other celebrities who shunned publicity, but this seemed over the top.

Another twenty minutes of searching brought her a meager reward in the form of a ten-year-old interview with Ms. Middlefield, but no photograph of the author accompanied the article. The only companion artwork was the cover of one of the medieval books. Sarah printed out the article and read it. The writer mentioned up front that Marjory was camera shy. The questions she'd answered centered on the book that had just been released at the time of the interview.

A nebulous idea was forming in her mind, but Sarah didn't want to jump to conclusions. She scoured the piece for clues. All she needed was one hint. Where did Ms. Middlefield live? How old was she? Where had she attended college? Was she married? All she needed was one solid piece of information to help her trace the author.

In the last paragraph of the article, Sarah unearthed one little nugget. Ms. Middlefield had recently moved back to her native New England. Although New England covered six states, Sarah started to get excited. Here was someone who had left New England and later returned, and had written a fictional story very much like Alice Ward's life.

Jumping up from her chair, Sarah hurried to where she'd left her purse and pulled out the little notebook she'd carried with her to Concord. The folded copy of Robert Ward's funeral program fell out, and she bent to retrieve it.

If she couldn't find anything about Marjory Middlefield, perhaps she could learn more about Alice and her family. She searched for an obituary for Robert Ward first. She knew from past investigations that obituaries in the 1940s were different from modern ones. They often ran in the local news section of the paper, not on a page of their own. The lawyer's death notice might have run in the Boston papers, and she'd need to find out if the online archives went back that far. She could also look for Alice's wedding announcement. If the electronic newspaper archives didn't have that, certainly the state archives would have a record of her marriage. Her fingers flew over the keys.

"Hi! What are you up to tonight?"

Sarah jumped and looked up at Belle, who stood in the doorway. "Oh, hello." She looked at her watch. "I'm sorry. I got caught up in my research, and I didn't realize it was so late."

"That's okay. What's so riveting?"

"Alice Ward."

Belle smiled. "I thought so. Find anything?"

"I'm looking for her father's obituary." Sarah hesitated, then said carefully, "Belle, I've found a coincidence. An odd but very big coincidence."

"Oh?"

Sarah nodded. "It's a doozy. You know that book I've been reading—the one Vanessa Sawyer lent me?"

"Sure."

"The part I'm reading now is just before Pearl Harbor. There's a girl in the book—she's one of the main characters—and her parents bought her a car. It's the same make, model, and year that Alice Ward's father bought her. Even the same color."

Belle was silent for a good ten seconds. At last she said, "Well. Why do you think that is?"

"I'm afraid to say it. But I want to either prove or discredit my theory before I tell anyone."

"Yes. I can see why. You don't want to get Mr. Pickett's hopes up."

"His and Joan Nash's. She's rooting for me now, too, hoping I'll find Alice. If I get them all excited about this and then it turns out to be nothing more than a common car model in 1939 and a rather often-used plot of a rich girl attracted to a poor hoodlum, why, they'd be crushed."

"I'm sure they'd be devastated if there was nothing to it."

"Yes. So I'm trying to uncover anything I can that will either substantiate my hunch or disprove it. I don't have a lot of facts. I do know when her father died and that Alice attended Radcliffe, then married a man named Russell Farmer in August, 1946. Not a lot besides that. I thought I'd try to find her father's obituary."

"And when is the last time you know for sure where she was?"

Sarah consulted her notes. "Russell and Alice moved to Colorado. Joan last heard from her in 1951."

Belle nodded. "So, instead of looking for her father's death records, why not look for something about Alice or her husband in Colorado?"

"That's not a bad idea. I can start with Colorado newspapers. Thank you, Belle. I believe I'll check major papers in Denver and see who has searchable archives."

Belle smiled. "I'll call you when the tea is ready."

Not until almost noon on Wednesday did Sarah hit pay dirt. She had done as much online searching as she could and had finally resorted to telephoning a few Denver newspapers. The archivist of one offered to help her and e-mailed her a short scanned article and an obituary.

Thunderstruck, Sarah read them, printed them, and read them again. In her hand she held Russell Farmer's obituary and a brief newspaper article about the accident that took his life and that of his three-year-old daughter Eleanor.

Sarah's heart ached. One line particularly grabbed her and made her feel ill.

Mrs. Farmer was also a passenger in the car at the time of the accident. No hint was given of Mrs. Farmer's condition.

Sarah called the newspaper again, but the librarian was unable to find a follow-up.

"We don't have the morgue information from back then computerized," the woman told her. "There might have been another notice, but no one filed it."

Absently, Sarah fixed herself a salad and a sandwich. Did Alice Farmer survive the accident? Joan had not heard the news of Russell Farmer's death or that of the little girl. Could Alice have been injured in the accident and succumbed afterward? And if she'd died in 1951, who wrote the story so closely paralleling her own? Obviously someone who knew her well.

A renewed search of other Colorado newspapers for an obituary for Alice Farmer turned up nothing. At last Sarah leaned back in her chair, rubbing her eyes. She considered the possibility that author Marjory Middlefield was someone who knew Alice Ward. Maybe working on the quilt would take her mind off things for a bit. She shut her computer down and got to work.

Snow fell that afternoon, and after basting the quilt top to the batting and plaid backing, Sarah sat down to finish reading *Before the Storm*. Riley argued violently with Ellie's father, and the older man took a punch at him. Riley swung back. Ellie's father fell and struck his head on the flag-stoned patio. Riley fled.

Sarah read avidly on. Ellie found Riley that evening and told him that her father was hospitalized and her mother was considering pressing charges. The two quarreled bitterly over her family's attitude. Ellie cried but refused to let him comfort her. Riley concluded that he and Ellie could never get past her parents' feelings or what had happened between him and her father. The next day he enlisted in the army. Ellie grieved over the painful separation. The next time she heard from him, it was a letter from France.

After she had turned the last page, Sarah sat looking out the front window for a long time. The author hadn't tied up all the loose ends of the story neatly, but the reader was left with hope that the two young lovers would have at least an even chance of a happy life together in the chaotic post-war world. Riley had reached out from the battlefield and begged Ellie's forgiveness, and she had responded with contrition and cautious hope. That was much more optimistic than Alice and Vern's real life story. Perhaps there was no connection.

At last Sarah stirred herself and called Joan Nash.

"What a pleasant surprise," Joan said. "Dare I hope that you've found something?"

"A little. I learned that Alice's husband Russell died in 1951."

"Oh no." Joan's voice fell. "The poor thing."

"Yes. Her little girl was killed in the same accident."

"Poor Alice. How very sad."

"It is. And Alice was in the car with them. I haven't been able to determine whether or not she was injured. I found Russell Farmer's obituary, and when it appeared in the newspaper, Alice was still alive, possibly in a hospital. I haven't found anything after that."

"You *will* keep me posted, if you learn anything else?"

Sarah leaned back in her chair, considering if she should ask Joan whether Alice could have been a writer. "Joan, you've told me Alice was a good student. Did she ever write stories when she was younger?"

"Not that I remember, other than school assignments."

"Did she like English class?"

"I suppose so, but she excelled at math. I do remember that she loved geography too."

Sarah sighed, her hopes wilting. "I have a reading assignment for you. They probably have it at the Concord Public Library. You might be able to find it in a book shop, though it's an older title. *Before the Storm*, by Marjory Middlefield. You need to read this book. Soon. And then call me and tell me what you think."

"All right." Joan sounded a bit mystified, but Sarah didn't want to say any more at the risk of influencing her impressions. If Joan read the novel and thought the similarities were merely coincidental, maybe Sarah could put her un-settling theory to rest.

On Thursday, Sarah did some more work on her bimonthly column for *Country Cottage*. The editor, Chester, had praised her first article, but her nerves still kicked in when she sat down to write. She'd never considered herself a writer—more of a craftsperson. But she always enjoyed telling people about her quilting adventures.

By Friday, she caught herself fidgeting as she went about her morning routine. Once she started to put on her coat, determined to go to Bradford Manor and see if she could get any more answers from Vern, but then she realized that there probably wasn't anything else he could add to their previous conversations.

She fixed herself a cup of tea and spent some extra time going over her article about making an heirloom quilt. Sarah hoped readers would be inspired to make a special quilt for their own families.

After noon, she went to her sewing machine and took out Vern's quilt. If she wasn't interrupted, she might be able to finish quilting it that day.

She'd only quilted one row when the telephone rang. Sarah's pulse quickened as she caught the excitement in Joan Nash's voice.

"Sarah! I can't believe it. I read several passages to Donald out loud last night, and he thinks the same as I do."

"The car," Sarah said.

"Yes, the car. The drugstore, the description of the old school. Everything. Even the way Ellie's father disapproved so strongly of Riley, the 'bad boy' Ellie fell in love with. Of course, most of that could be explained away as part of the common experience of New England teenagers in the early '40s."

"How did Mr. Ward learn she was seeing Vern?" Sarah asked.

"He saw them together. He was going to his office and saw Alice's car coming down the street—with Vern at the wheel and Alice sitting very close to him."

"I guess that upset her father."

"Yes. He forbade Alice to see Vern anymore. She cried and cried. They met on the sly after that. Finally Vern went to see Mr. Ward. He didn't want to give up seeing Alice, and he was willing to try to talk it out with her father."

"But Mr. Ward wasn't agreeable?"

"No," Joan said. "He threw him out of the house. Not literally, but Alice overheard what he said. Her father told Vern not to imagine he would ever be good enough for Alice."

"How sad. In the book, Riley and Ellie's father came to blows."

"Yes, but that didn't happen in real life. Dramatic license, I guess. But there were two things in the story that clinched it for me. One was the necklace."

"Necklace? Oh, the pendant Ellie's best friend gave her."

"Yes! Don't you see? I'm Diane. I have to be. The necklace that Diane gave to Ellie for a graduation present is identical to the one I gave Alice on our graduation day. Right down to the marcasite chips in the setting around the amethyst."

"What's the other thing?"

"Page 213."

"Oh? What was that?" Vanessa's book was in the living room, where Sarah had left it.

"The bridge incident," Joan said. "Alice came and tapped on my window at eleven-thirty one night. She scared me about to death. She'd sneaked out to meet Vern down near the river. They were wading or something, and somehow she fell in. Or he threw her in. I don't know—put exuberant kids near water and someone's bound to get wet, right?"

Sarah laughed.

"So Alice knocked on my window, begging for dry clothes in the middle of the night."

"So that really happened?"

"Yes, and I've never told anyone about it. I don't think I'd even told that story to Donald. Whoever Marjory Middlefield is, she knew Alice. Very, very well."

CHAPTER TWELVE

Sarah tried not to get too excited. "There are other possibilities."

"Like what?" Joan asked.

"Even though you kept Alice's secrets, she might have told someone else later on. Or she could have written about those things in her diary, and years later someone else read it and used the basic story in a book."

"You're right." Joan's tone sagged. "I didn't think about that. I suppose Alice could have remarried after Russell died. She could even have married a writer, or told a friend or a caregiver about her high school days."

"Yes, any of those situations is possible," Sarah said. "But there's also another way it could have happened. It's a little wild, so I hesitate to mention it."

"What? Tell me!"

"You said Vern was a pretty good writer in high school."

"Vern?" Joan said nothing for a few seconds. "You're not serious. I mean, yes, he wrote poems, but I don't know how good they were. You don't really think he . . . " She gave a little moan.

"Vern would have known about the bridge incident," Sarah pointed out. "Would he know about the necklace?"

"I don't know. Maybe. In fact, I'd say probably." Joan paused. "So, we can't discount the remote possibility that Vern, or someone close to him, wrote this novel. What can we do to find out who this author really is?"

"I'm trying to discover more about Marjory Middlefield. I've located one article online that was written in 2001. It said Marjory Middlefield had moved back to New England."

"So she was from here originally?"

Sarah thought. "Well, it could be an accidental turn of phrase—or it could mean many places other than Massachusetts. But I have an idea of what I can do next."

"Tell me before I explode all over my living room."

Sarah chuckled. "Oh, don't do that. You'll ruin that lovely carpet. I have a dear friend here in Maple Hill who just bought the newest book by Marjory Middlefield a few days ago. I'll see if there's an address where readers can write to the author, or I'll try to contact her through the publisher."

"What a fantastic idea. Oh, Sarah, you'll do it soon, won't you?"

"Yes. In fact, I'll do it today if I can."

Sarah walked into the fabric shop half an hour later. Vanessa was with a customer, so Sarah strolled to the book and magazine display and browsed the monthly craft magazines. She loved the store—the bright fabrics and yarns, the plain old sewing tools and the fancy new gadgets. Even the smell of the shop drew her. A few minutes later, the customer paid for her purchases and left. Vanessa hurried to Sarah's side.

"What's up, lady? Run out of thread again?"

"No, I'm here on a different errand," Sarah said. She put the magazine she'd been browsing back in the rack. "Would you possibly have that new book you bought last week here with you?"

"I sure do. I nearly finished it last night, but I fell asleep. Naturally the one day I want to read is the busiest day I've had since Christmas."

"Well, that's good. I'm glad business has picked up."

"So, you want to borrow it? As soon as I—"

"Oh no," Sarah said quickly. "I don't need to take it out of the store. I just want to *look* at it."

Vanessa eyed her closely, and Sarah could see that she needed to explain. By the time she'd recounted all the similarities she and Joan had found in *Before the Storm* and Alice's real life, Vanessa was staring at her in disbelief.

"That is the craziest thing I've ever heard."

"I know. I figure Marjory Middlefield must have a close connection to Alice."

The bell jingled as two women entered the store.

"Hello, ladies," Vanessa called to them. "I'll be right with you." To Sarah, she said, "The book's under the counter. Come on over."

"Great." Sarah followed her to the counter. Vanessa went behind the cash register and pulled out her hardback copy of *The Celtic Courtship*.

"Don't lose my place." Vanessa grinned at her and went to wait on the newcomers.

Sarah opened the book and skimmed the front matter. It had been published by a large publishing house in New York. She saw nothing about the author, so she flipped to the back. Ads for several more of Ms. Middlefield's titles splashed across the last few pages, but she found no biographical note or letter to the reader, as she had seen in some other authors' books. With a sigh she took out her notebook and wrote down the publishing information.

Vanessa walked past her with a bolt of fabric. "Find what you need?"

"Yes, thank you, Vanessa."

She drove home and went to her computer. The publishing house's Web site featured Marjory Middlefield's new book on its home page. Sarah checked for information about the author but found only a list of Marjory's books published by that house. She printed it out, then searched for a way to contact the publisher. The screen confronted her with a choice of e-mail, phone number, or mailing address.

She tapped her pen against her lips. E-mail would be quickest and least painful. But could she hope for a quick reply? And if the answer came but was unsatisfactory, what would she do then? She decided to telephone. E-mails could so easily be misconstrued.

Her call was answered cheerfully by a receptionist, and Sarah tried to frame her request as simply as possible.

"I'd like to speak to someone who can give me some information about Marjory Middlefield's work."

"One moment while I transfer you to Editorial."

Sarah sat drumming her fingers on the desk and wondered if she was on the right track or if she would just get caught in a circle of voice mails.

"Andrea Becker. May I help you?"

"Hello." Sarah sat up straight, as though the businesslike woman on the other end could see her. "My name is Sarah Hart, and I'm looking for information about Marjory Middlefield."

"What exactly do you want to know?"

"Where she lives?"

"I'm sorry. I can't give you that information."

Sarah repressed a sigh. "Of course you can't. Forgive me, I realize you're not allowed to give out personal information. Would it be too personal to tell me what state Ms. Middlefield lives in?"

After a slight pause, Ms. Becker asked, "Are you writing an article?"

"No, nothing like that. Oh dear, I should have started by telling you my purpose. I'm trying to help two friends find an old schoolmate, Alice Ward, and in one of Ms. Middlefield's books, she describes some incidents that are identical to events that occurred in Alice Ward's life. We believe Ms. Middlefield must have known Alice well, and my friends would dearly like to renew their friendship. I assure you there is nothing sinister about it. They're both elderly people, and they care deeply for Alice."

Another pause, longer than the last.

"And where are you calling from?"

Sarah exhaled. At least she hadn't been summarily rejected. "I live in Maple Hill, Massachusetts, and one of my friends also lives here. The other lives in Concord."

"And you said they were childhood friends of someone in a book?"

"Yes. Schoolmates of the heroine in Ms. Middlefield's first book, *Before the Storm*. And they would like—"

"But the heroine is a fictional character."

"Yes, I realize that, but we believe she is based on the real Alice Ward."

"Well … let me see … "

Again Sarah waited, expecting to be disconnected any moment. She scribbled *Andrea Becker* on her notebook, so she wouldn't forget whom she'd spoken with if she had to call again. At last Ms. Becker came back on the line.

"Hello, Ms. Hart?"

"Yes," Sarah said.

"I'm going to transfer you to one of our fiction editors, Karen Zilt. She works closely with Ms. Middlefield, and I think she's better suited to help you than I am."

Sarah smiled. "Thank you very much." At last. She felt she was on the verge of a breakthrough. When Karen Zilt came on the line, she tried to explain her mission succinctly.

"I'm sure you realize that we can't give out personal information about our authors," Ms. Zilt said.

"Oh, of course." Sarah pressed on. "It's just that my friend, Joan Nash, is certain that Ms. Middlefield must know the old friend she lost contact with many years ago. She recently read *Before the Storm*, and there are things in that book that Joan says happened to her and friend. Things only a handful of people knew about. And the author wrote about a necklace the character Diane gave to Ellie in the book, and Joan says it's identical to the necklace she gave her friend. Only a few people would know that. She's very excited about the possibility of finding Alice again."

"Alice?" Ms. Zilt said.

"Alice Ward. That was her friend's name. Mrs. Nash thinks—and to be honest, so do I—that Marjory Middlefield must have been friends with her old classmate, or possibly even a family member of Alice's writing under the pen name Marjory Middlefield. Someone close to Alice, at any rate."

After one of those interminable pauses Sarah had come to loathe, Ms. Zilt said, "I'm sorry, but I can't confirm or deny any of this. Ms. Middlefield is a very private person. She doesn't give interviews anymore; she doesn't even allow photos on her book covers. When she receives mail here, we *do* pass it on to her. I suggest that you write or e-mail here to the office, and we'll see that she gets it as soon as possible."

Sarah fought back her disappointment.

Karen Zilt gave Sarah her e-mail address, and Sarah wrote it down and read it back to her. "That's correct. I'll watch for your message and make sure that Ms. Middlefield receives it."

"Thank you so much." Sarah laid down the phone and immediately opened her e-mail account. After several false starts, she wrote a concise, yet kind e-mail, explaining to Ms. Middlefield that she hoped the author could help her find an old friend, Alice Ward. She read it over once more, then hit send, praying that the e-mail would make its way to Ms. Middlefield as soon as possible.

She laid the notebook beside the computer and put Alice's picture on top of it for inspiration. The tattered edges of the photo reminded her of all Vern had gone through while he carried it. If Vern was being honest with her, she really ought to tell him where her investigation had taken her and make sure he wanted to pursue this. But what if he wasn't telling her the whole truth? And what if Alice was out there, but didn't want to be found?

Sarah thought about the small details she knew from Vern's background. He had a bad memory, but that hadn't always been the case. He'd had a wife who would have heard his old stories many times. He'd also had friends in the army and in school. How much of his courtship of Alice had he revealed to Bob Willis, for instance? And then there was his sister Nora. When it came down to it, a lot of people might know about this ill-fated high school love.

With sudden resolution, she pushed her chair back. She was procrastinating only because she didn't want to confront Vern again. But she couldn't hold off any longer.

She drove first to The Spotted Dog. To her disappointment, Liam did not have a copy of *Before the Storm* in stock.

"I can get that in for you inside of a week," he said.

"Good. Get me two copies, please." She would keep one herself. By the time they arrived, she'd have to decide whether or not to give the other to Vern. Depending on what she found out in the meantime, that might be too painful a gift—or a ridiculous one.

"All right. Now, will you be wanting a drink today?"

Sarah smiled. "Thanks, Liam, but I have another errand. Maybe tomorrow." She said good-bye to him and patted Murphy on her way out the door.

As always, at the nursing home she peeked into her father's room first. Vern sat in his wheelchair, and William in his recliner. On William's rolling tray table was a checkerboard.

"Hi, Dad." Sarah gave him a big smile.

"That's my girl, Sarah," her father said to Vern.

Vern nodded. "Yes, we've met. She's a very nice lady."

Sarah relaxed and went to sit on the bed. Her father appeared to be having a good day, and she appreciated the low-key attention Vern was giving him.

"What are you up to today?" William asked.

"Just running a few errands, and I thought I'd drop in to see you. Who's winning?"

"Hmm. Not sure."

Sarah smiled and turned to Vern. "I drove over to Concord Monday."

Vern paused with his hand over the checkerboard and eyed her curiously. "Oh? So, you followed through with it."

"Yes. I had lunch with Joan Franklin Nash."

"Is she a friend of yours?" William asked.

Vern sat back and let his hand fall to his lap. "I suppose you could say that." He turned to Sarah. "How is she?"

"She's great. Very spry. She and her husband Donald have a lovely home there in town. And she remembers you."

Vern nodded slowly. "Yeah? What about ... Alice?"

Sarah shook her head. "Joan didn't have an address for her. I hope to find out more soon." She watched him closely. "Have you ever heard of a writer named Marjory Middlefield?"

"I don't think so. What does she write?"

"Mostly historical romance novels."

He laughed. "Not my usual reading material."

Vern hadn't shown any surprise or recognition. No clue that he might know about the writer who had so vividly described his life. "No, I suppose not. I hadn't read any of her books until recently, but she's been around for a while and has more than thirty books in print."

"Oh?" Vern didn't really sound interested.

"Yes. One of her books is set in Massachusetts in 1940 and 1941." Despite his lack of reaction, Sarah continued. "And there were some things in the book ... " She decided to take the plunge. "Vern, the girl in the book had a blue 1939 Chevy."

His forehead wrinkled, but he said nothing.

"She also received a gift of an amethyst necklace that's exactly like one Joan gave Alice on their graduation day."

Vern swallowed hard. "What are you saying?"

"I'm not sure yet. I've contacted the editor in New York. There were other things in the book, too—things Joan recognized that I didn't. There was something she said happened to her and Alice, but they'd never told anyone about it. At least, Joan hadn't. But maybe Alice did, and this person wrote about it."

"You think that's what happened? Alice told somebody about her time in high school, and they wrote a book about it?"

Sarah pressed her lips together. "Vern, I think this author is someone who was close to Alice. But in that case, Alice would have told this person things about her teenage years that nobody else knew but Joan. Or you."

"Me?"

"Like the night you and Alice met down near the Concord River and Alice fell in the water. Do you remember that?"

He stared at her for a moment. "How could anyone forget something like that?" He smiled, but he looked a little worried.

Sarah was tempted to press him further for details. "Joan remembered Alice going to her window in the dark and asking her to help her get dry clothes before she went home."

"Was I with her?" he asked softly. He glanced at Sarah. "I mean ... to be honest I don't remember all the details. I guess we were horsing around, but when Alice fell in, she was sure her folks would be mad. That must have been it. Her father had quite a temper."

"Did you go with her to Joan's? Did you leave her there, so you wouldn't be seen together if either Joan's parents or Alice's saw you?"

"That must be what happened." Vern sat very still, staring at the checkerboard. After a long minute he shot her an anxious look. "What if somebody else stole her story? What if she told them this stuff and they just ... you know, lifted it."

"It's a possibility. Alice may have died a long time ago, and she certainly could have told a relative or a caretaker about those things before she died, or left a journal that told about them. But anyway, I'm working on it. I hope we can get a conclusive answer."

"Me too." He eyed her cautiously. "Is there any possibility Alice wrote that book herself?"

"I suppose so. But she's your age—and Marjorie Middle-field is still writing novels. I guess it's possible, but don't hope too hard, okay?"

He licked his lips. "If she's gone, this author would know."

"I think so."

"But if she's alive, why hasn't she talked to any of her old friends for so long?"

"I don't know. I wrote to Ms. Middlefield in care of her publisher. But be prepared for an answer saying she doesn't want to have anything to do with me or Joan—or you."

"But if she's Alice—"

"We may never know who she is," Sarah said. "If she's writing under a pen name and wants to maintain her anonymity...could you handle that?"

"I..." He swiveled his chair a bit so that he faced her directly. "I need to know if she's alive. I've got something I have to tell her. I promised myself if I ever found her again..."

Sarah patted his arm. "All right. I'll let you know when I hear back from the publisher. And if we get hit with a big disappointment, we'll face it together."

Sarah glanced at her father to see how much of this he was taking in. William watched them with apparent interest. "Vern, I'll do everything I can."

CHAPTER THIRTEEN

Dear Marjory Middlefield,

I recently finished reading your book Before the Storm, and I enjoyed it tremendously. In fact, I recommended it to a friend, Joan (Franklin) Nash. When she read the book, Joan was surprised to find some things that made her believe she knows you or someone close to you. Joan graduated from Concord High School in 1942, and her classmate and dear friend Alice Ward graduated with her. They lost contact a few years later, and Joan would like to reunite with Alice. I am also acquainted with a gentleman named Vern Pickett, who cared deeply about Alice Ward. He, too, would like to know what became of her.

If you can help, please let me know as soon as possible. We respect your desire for privacy, but I'm hoping you can help these dear people who have waited many years to learn more about their old friend.

Sincerely,
Sarah Hart

Sarah re-read her e-mail, now housed in the "Sent" items folder. There had been no new messages when she got back from the nursing home, though she knew she shouldn't hope for a response so soon.

Lord, thy will be done.

A cup of tea was in order. Sarah went to the kitchen and took her time preparing it. When she returned to the computer, she noticed that a message with Karen Zilt's "from" address had appeared. She set her mug of tea down and opened the e-mail.

"Mrs. Hart, While the author seldom engages in personal correspondence, be assured your letter has been passed on to Ms. Middlefield."

Sarah shot off a quick "Thank you," and returned to her quilting project. Working with the colorful old fabrics and the sturdy thread calmed her. While she worked, she thought about what she would do the next day. Maybe she could do a little more sleuthing, but she should shop, too. She'd offered to pick up any groceries and sundries Pastor John wanted, and he'd asked her to call Saturday morning to see what he needed. Martha hadn't called her for several days, and Sarah hoped that meant she'd found volunteers for the tasks that still needed to be done. As she continued to snip and sew, she prayed for Pastor John, for Martha and Ernie, and for Vern, Joan, and Alice.

Lord, if Marjory Middlefield does know Alice, please let her see that it would be cruel not to let Vern and Joan learn that, and reveal whatever she knows about Alice.

Although Vern's surprise at her news had seemed genuine, Sarah still had a nagging feeling that something wasn't right where he was concerned. His selective memory at times seemed too convenient. She couldn't shake the feeling that he was holding something back. Maybe Scott could put her mind at ease.

McKenna greeted her cordially at seven o'clock that evening, though she seemed a bit guarded.

"Come in, Mrs. Hart. I'll tell Scott you're here."

She took Sarah's jacket and hat, then walked toward an open doorway. Before she reached it, Scott came through it carrying his son.

"Hi, Mrs. Hart."

"Thank you for agreeing to see me on short notice."

"No problem. Have a seat."

Sarah sat on the sofa, and McKenna took a rocking chair, watching Caleb. The little boy wriggled in his father's arms, and Scott let him down on the braided rug as he sat in the only armchair in the room.

"What can I help you with?" Scott asked.

"I just had a couple more questions. I wondered if Vern has a computer."

"No, he's never done much with computers," McKenna replied.

Sarah nodded and asked Scott, "Would you say that your grandfather is much of a writer? I'm told that in high school he wanted to be a writer. He wrote poems."

Scott laughed. "Grandpa? I can't imagine it."

"So he's never written out any stories...or memories, perhaps?"

Scott shook his head.

"A journal, maybe?"

"What's this about?" He cocked his head to one side, his forehead furrowed. Caleb tugged at his hands, and Scott absently pulled back.

"I've found Alice Ward's best friend, Joan. Some of the things she's told me about high school don't add up."

"Do you think she's lying?" McKenna asked.

Sarah hesitated, thinking of the inconsistencies she'd noticed. "Somebody is."

Scott frowned. "What are you saying? Grandpa's a liar?"

"No, I didn't mean that." Sarah sighed. "I'm sorry. I didn't mean to upset you. I'm only trying to find out the truth. It could be that fuzzy memories and old age are to blame."

"I don't see how we can do anything about that." Scott lifted Caleb onto his lap.

"You may be right." Her gaze fell on the photo she'd seen the first time she visited. "Do you have any pictures of your grandfather when he was young?"

"You mean, like his wedding pictures?" Scott asked.

"Earlier than that. Childhood pictures."

He shook his head. "He told me that when his mother died, Aunt Nora cleaned out the house. He was in the VA hospital, so I guess she took everything like that."

"There's that one over there." McKenna rose and took the picture of Vern and his buddy off the bookcase.

Sarah studied it closely. A dark spot marred a small portion of the image, obscuring Vern's left sleeve and part of his torso, but his face was clear. Scott came over and looked over her shoulder, holding Caleb against his side. Scott cleared his throat. "Do you seriously think Grandpa's been lying to you about Alice Ward? I mean, what would be the point?"

"I'm not sure."

Before going shopping on Saturday afternoon, Sarah decided to drop in and pay a brief call on Martha. Her friend opened the door and threw her arms around Sarah.

"I'm so glad to see you. Come in!"

"Is everything all right?" Sarah entered and unzipped her jacket.

"Yes, I suppose so, but I'm overwhelmed. So many things have come up this week that had to be done for the church. If I could, I would get someone to take care of it without mentioning it to Pastor John, so he wouldn't feel bad about it. I had to call him at least half a dozen times. Poor man!" Martha took the jacket and hung it in the coat closet.

"Don't let it get you down," Sarah said. "You've done a fantastic job, and the pastor is getting better. It won't be long before he can take over all his duties again. And if you can't handle something, the rest of us members owe you support. I'm sure you've been doing too much."

Martha sighed and turned toward the kitchen. "Let's have tea. I was just going over my lists and making sure I had everything covered for tomorrow."

"Let me take a look too," Sarah said. "If we need to get someone else in on it, we will."

While Martha prepared the tea, Sarah sat down at the table and looked over three sheets of printed paper. "Oh my, you have had a lot to deal with. You've been picking up the church mail?"

"I got the secretary to take that over. And she said she'd call John to see what hymns he wanted for tomorrow's service."

"Good." Sarah picked up the second list. "Aha. You've crossed off 'pick up pastor before church.'"

"Yes, Jason offered to get John and his wheelchair tomorrow morning in Maggie's SUV."

"Terrific. I'm so glad John feels up to preaching. But what's this sheet?"

Martha came over and looked over her shoulder. "Oh, that one."

The discouraged tone in her voice made Sarah turn to study her face. "What's wrong?"

"That's the list of all the people I've asked to pick up the missionary speaker. Nobody wants to drive to Logan, and the excuses are getting thinner and more ridiculous."

Sarah counted the names on the sheet of paper. "Wow. You've asked eleven people, and they all said no?"

"That's right. And some of those are couples who both turned me down." Martha brought their mugs over to the table. "Here's your tea."

"It shouldn't be this hard, should it?" Sarah asked.

Martha's face scrunched up. "My head says you're right, but then I look at these lists..."

"This has been a huge job."

"Yes. But I've learned some things from it."

"Such as?"

"Such as, don't call the Londons' house before nine in the morning."

Sarah chuckled.

"No, seriously, I've learned that when you're responsible, that's the bottom line. Even if other people don't want to help, you have to get things done." Martha took a sip of her tea. Sarah lifted her mug and took a cautious sip. "Mm. Delicious."

"Thanks. It's raspberry."

Sarah looked over the paper again. "Hmm...dental appointment, babysitting grandchildren, having car detailed, dog grooming appointment."

"I told you some of the excuses were flimsy. It's the long drive on winter roads, I think."

"Maybe we should make a list of all the people who haven't said no yet."

"I'm not sure that would help." Just as Martha spoke, her kitchen phone rang. She jumped up to answer it. "Oh, hello, Mike. Thanks for calling back. I'm looking for somebody to pick up our missionary speaker for church a week from Friday. He's flying in to Logan."

While she talked, Sarah glanced at the third sheet. It was Martha's list of people taking meals to the pastor. The

Maplethorpes were having John in for dinner following the Sunday service, and Martha seemed to have lunch and supper cooks lined up through Tuesday.

"Oh, I'm sorry to hear that." Martha said into the phone.

Sarah turned toward her and waited, listening.

"Your son made the finals in the snowboarding competition," Martha said. "I see. Of course the whole family should go and cheer him on. Give Mickey my congratulations."

When she had hung up, Sarah said, "So, I guess that was number twelve."

"Yup." Martha sat down and reached for her mug.

Sarah sank back in her chair. "And you've been going through this sort of thing every day?"

"Not this bad." Martha got up again and put the teakettle back on the burner. "Our tea is getting cold."

"I could probably do it, you know," Sarah said. "Drive to Boston, that is."

"No. You've done plenty. That's another thing I've learned over the past two weeks: a handful of people have been doing most of the jobs. It would be good to get more people involved. They'll bless others and get a blessing themselves. But there are a few who refuse to do anything. Too busy." Martha shook her head and sighed. "I shouldn't be upset. He's got a business, and I'm sure he felt he truly couldn't help. But I look at people like you and Jason and Harry Butler, who've done so much ... Well, I'm keeping you here while I moan and complain, and you've got other fish to fry."

Sarah hugged her. "I do need to get to the store, but call me if you have another crisis."

At quarter past six, Sarah walked wearily into her kitchen carrying two sacks of groceries. Belle sat at the table eating. A couple of white food cartons sat on the countertop.

"Hello! Have you had supper?" Belle asked.

"No," Sarah said. "I do have more groceries in the car."

"I'll help." Belle grabbed her jacket from a hook by the back door. "I bought some egg rolls and General Tso's chicken on my way home. I took a chance and got enough for two."

"Wonderful!" Sarah hadn't realized how tired she was. After they'd brought in her purchases, she got a plate, a fork, and a glass of water, and sat down opposite Belle. "Thank you for doing this."

"No problem. I called an hour or so ago to see if you'd cooked, but you didn't answer, so I followed my hunch."

They finished dinner and were putting away the leftovers when Sarah's mind began to wander. As the last piece of silverware was dropped in the dishwasher, she went off to her sewing room.

She closed the curtains and turned on the computer. No e-mail from Marjory Middlefield, or her editor Ms. Zilt. But a familiar name showed up in her in-box. Sarah opened it and quickly downloaded the file attachment. The old photograph that appeared made her smile.

Two girls stood in front of an old car. As Sarah suspected, Joan's message confirmed that this was the famous 1939

Chevy that had played a part in causing the rift between the young sweethearts.

"I'm sorry I couldn't find a photo of Vern," Joan had typed. "There's a tiny headshot of him in one yearbook, but I couldn't scan it so that it was recognizable. I don't think you saw this one on Monday. It was taken right after Alice got the car."

Sarah e-mailed back: "That's all right. Thank you for trying. I love the picture you sent. You and Alice both look very happy."

She printed out the photo of Joan and Alice. It came out quite well, and she put it in the notebook dedicated to her search. In the back of the notebook was the reunion invitation she'd found in Vern's shirt pocket. She took it out and read it again. Would any of those men remember Vern if he went to the gathering? She noted the e-mail contact at the bottom of the page. She sucked in a deep breath, squared her shoulders, and began to type a new message.

CHAPTER FOURTEEN

<hr />

After dinner at Jason and Maggie's on Sunday, Sarah again opened the photo of Alice and Joan standing in front of Alice's car on her computer screen. It was much clearer than the printout, and the girls' vibrant faces made her smile. She decided to pass it on. Quickly she attached it to an e-mail and typed in Karen Zilt's address.

Ms. Zilt, Joan Nash sent me this picture of herself and her old friend, Alice Ward, taken in 1941. I wondered if you might please send it to Marjory Middlefield and tell her that Alice Ward's old friend, Joan Franklin Nash, would dearly love to know what happened to Alice and how her story came to be told in Before the Storm.

She read through it again.

Sending the picture seemed the right thing to do. She clicked on Send and exhaled.

After the message had gone, the chime sounded for incoming e-mail. Sarah drew in a deep breath. The retired sergeant in charge of the Massachusetts 182nd had replied to her inquiry.

Thanks for your note, Mrs. Hart. I remember Vern, though I wasn't in Guadalcanal at the time he was wounded. I met him later, when our unit was sent to Bougainville. He'd been laid up for a while was my understanding. I didn't get to know him very well, but we'd love to see him again. He'll get a big welcome if he comes to the reunion. I've attached a photo of some of the men from his platoon from last year's reunion.

She opened the picture and studied the wrinkled faces. These men were bound together by the horrible experience they'd shared. She read the names, but she didn't know which ones Vern would recognize. Remembering the photo at Scott's house, she searched the faces again, looking for the tall man who'd stood next to Vern in the snapshot, but she couldn't pinpoint him.

Her instinct was to print out the picture and take it to Vern, but something held her back. Instead, she opened a new e-mail and began to type.

On Monday, Sarah did laundry and a little dusting, then worked on Vern's pillow sham until noon. When it was finished, she pressed it and folded it carefully. She placed it and the finished quilt in a large plastic bag. She hoped when she took it to him, she could also take him some promising news about Alice, but that might not happen.

After lunch, she settled down to work at the computer. With Belle at work, the house was very quiet. She'd considered advertising for another boarder, but had put it off. The Lord had a way of sending women to her when they needed a place to live.

The first thing she searched for was the Americal Division. The unit had been formed in 1942 out of several state National Guard units. Vern's regiment, the Massachusetts 182nd, joined with the 164th of North Dakota and the 132nd of Illinois. The new division was named for America and New Caledonia—the place where it was organized and christened.

Sarah read a brief summary of the unit's service. Guadalcanal and Bougainville were two of the major engagements for the Americal Division. Everything Vern had told her seemed to line up correctly with what she read.

She frowned over the timeline. He'd said he went straight from boot camp to New Caledonia. If he'd enlisted early in December 1941, there seemed to be several months unaccounted for. The Americal's formation didn't happen until the following May. Would basic training take that long in wartime? Vern had spoken of delays due to the lack of operational ships. Probably the men were shuttled about for several weeks before they arrived in New Caledonia.

She supposed it was a very traumatic time for him, and his memories of the war remained vivid. His commanding officers and army buddies had been with him at the most harrowing time of his life, unlike the folks from his dreamlike adolescence in Concord. She wished he could pull out a few more details about Alice and her family, but she didn't want to push too much.

She roamed away from the grim accounts of warfare. Next she read several online reviews of Marjory Middlefield's novels. More than a dozen of her books had hit the *New York Times* bestseller list. Two had been made into movies. The author's work certainly struck a chord with many readers. But for all her searching, Sarah could not turn up more personal information about Ms. Middlefield. She must have someone watchdogging for her, to make sure her name didn't show up on Web sites designed to help people locate others. Usually a determined amateur could find someone's telephone number and address online. All Sarah found were routes back to the publisher.

She couldn't even find evidence to confirm the author's age. She tried to piece it together, but she had no clue earlier than the copyright date of *Before the Storm*—1952.

Finally she turned away from the computer.

Lord, I feel as though I'm wasting time. Please help me realize that this whole search is worthwhile.

On Tuesday, Sarah at last received the call she'd longed for from Karen Zilt.

"I'm sorry we kept you waiting, Mrs. Hart, but I wanted to be sure Ms. Middlefield had time to absorb your message, and that she understood your intentions."

Sarah tried not to hold her breath. "Thank you for calling," she murmured. "Did you receive the picture I sent Sunday?"

"Yes, I did. It's a charming photograph. In fact, I think seeing it swayed Marjory. She'd like to meet with you and Joan Nash."

Sarah nearly gasped. How far would they have to go to meet her? Hundreds of miles, or up the hill to Bradford Manor?

Karen Zilt went on, "She asked me to extend an invitation to you ladies to take tea with her at her home in Lexington."

"Lexington, Massachusetts?"

"That's right."

"How wonderful." A thousand questions filled her mind. When could they go? How could Marjory live so close and no one in the area seemed to know? And would the author have asked to meet Joan and Sarah if she hadn't been really close to Alice Ward? She ventured, "Did she specify a time?"

"Tomorrow, if you're able. If that's too soon—"

"No, it's perfect. Of course, I'll have to confirm with Joan, but I'm free, and the weather should be fine. I'd be happy to pick Joan up and take her to Lexington."

"Excellent." Karen gave her the address. "It would be best if you arrived around two o'clock. And I'll give you the phone number to call if anything unexpected comes up and prevents you from being there. This is Marjory's personal assistant's number."

Sarah wrote it down carefully. "May I ask, did she say anything about Mr. Pickett? He especially wants to know what happened to Alice Ward. If Ms. Middlefield knew her personally…"

"I'm sorry. I've been asked not to give too much information, and I respect Marjory's privacy. I think she will answer some of your questions. But she definitely asked to see only you and Mrs. Nash. I'm not sure whether or not she'll be open to meeting your other friend later."

"Of course. Thank you so much for doing this."

When they'd hung up, Sarah spent a moment in thought. Would Vern ever have a chance to give Alice the message he wanted so badly to deliver?

She took up the phone and eagerly punched in Joan's number, thankful that she could at last present some promising news to one of the elderly classmates.

"Joan, it's Sarah Hart. I've heard from Karen Zilt, the editor. Are you free tomorrow?"

"Tomorrow?" Joan asked. "Why, yes, I think so. I'll check with Donald. Are you coming to Concord again?"

"Yes, I am. To Concord and beyond. You and I have been invited to have tea with Marjory Middlefield."

"What? Where?"

"Lexington."

Joan's shout made Sarah pull the phone away from her ear for a second. "She has to know Alice! She wouldn't want to see an old nobody like me unless she had a reason."

"Oh, you silly thing. You're not a nobody. But yes, her invitation tells us she at least knows something about Alice."

"I'm so excited," Joan said.

"I'll pick you up at one, if that works for you."

"We'll have such fun, Sarah. Just think! Even if this writer never met Alice in person, I've been living less than twenty miles from a famous author for the last ten years and didn't know it."

"Well, Sarah! Haven't seen you for a while." Irene Stuart, the director of the Maple Hill Historical Society, was an old friend of Sarah's. Her charm bracelet clinked as she came to clasp Sarah's hand. "What can I help you with today?"

"I'm studying up on World War II. A certain army unit fought at Guadalcanal and took heavy fire from the enemy. I've done a little research on them, but I want more details about their experience. If possible, I'd like to prove or disprove something I was told."

"Oh? Sounds intriguing."

Sarah unfolded a printout of the second e-mail she'd received from the retired National Guard sergeant. "This is what a veteran who's connected with the regiment's reunion told me. '*Pickett's entire squad took a bad hit in the last days of combat on Guadalcanal. I understand he was the only survivor.*' So, my friend's the only one in his platoon who lived through that attack. No, wait." She glanced at the paper again. "Not his platoon, his squad. What's the difference between a platoon and a squad? And is there a way I can check that story?"

"Hmm." Irene's brow furrowed. "It should be easy to check on how many men were involved. And if he lived around here, we could look up newspaper accounts from the time, and we might be able to look up military records too. Is he still alive?"

"Yes, he's at Bradford Manor. And I should stipulate that I haven't asked him about it. I didn't want to bring it up in conversation with the man if it wasn't so. But this e-mail isn't official, and the battle was more than sixty years ago. I just want to check it out."

"I have only one project I'm working on today. I think I can give you an hour. And if we find some promising leads, Tim could keep working with you."

"That sounds good. Thank you." Tim Wexler was a high school student who worked part-time at the historical society. He'd helped Sarah before, and she was impressed with his intuition and diligence.

When Tim joined them, Sarah explained her search, and they went into the stacks. The society had a large collection of World War II resources, and they pulled books, maps, and folders that had to do with the Guadalcanal Campaign and laid them out on a long oak table.

By closing time they had found little specific information about Vern's unit—only that when the Americal Division was transported to Guadalcanal, the North Dakota regiment landed first. The other soldiers in the division came later, and were in the islands from October or November 1942 to February 1943.

"This all goes along with what Mr. Pickett told me," Sarah said. "His unit arriving late, as he put it, and being transported from New Caledonia. But it's not quite what I was looking for."

"I'm sorry, Mrs. Hart," Tim said. "I can keep working on this. Can you come back tomorrow? I'll come right over after school."

"I'm afraid not," Sarah said. "I'm driving to Lexington tomorrow. But I might be able to snatch an hour at the library in Concord."

"Sure." Tim grinned at her. "Your soldier lived in Concord, right? They might have something about him. That would be a good place to look. And I'll keep working on it here, unless Mrs. Stuart has another project for me tomorrow afternoon."

Sarah got to Concord a few minutes before she was due to pick up Joan. She'd decided to forgo the visit to the library until after the appointment with Marjory Middlefield. If time allowed, she could stop in then. If not, she might have to call Laura Baird again and request long distance help.

Sarah and Joan settled in Sarah's car for the drive to Lexington.

"I'll be so disappointed if we find out Alice is dead." Joan pulled her seat belt out and tugged it snugly across her middle.

"I'm trying not to fix my hopes too firmly," Sarah said.

Joan sighed. "I've always hoped that she was alive some-where and happy. She seemed such a tragic figure, and not knowing what happened caused me to imagine all sorts of dreadful things."

Sarah reached over and squeezed her hand. "I just hope I haven't brought more unhappiness into people's lives by poking into things. Joan, could we pray before we head over there?"

Joan gave her a shaky smile. "Oh yes!" They bowed their heads while Sarah said a brief prayer, then they were off.

Sarah drove cautiously, though the streets were clear of snow and well marked. They arrived at the address to find a gated stone wall between them and the house. Sarah pulled in to the stub of the driveway in front of the gate and stopped. Before she or Joan could voice their uncertainty, the gate swung open.

Sarah put the car in gear and let it roll through the gate and slowly up the paved driveway. A plow had left ridges of snow banks on both sides of the drive. A one-story stone house stood at the back of the large lot, set amid bare-limbed trees and snowy expanses that must be lawns and flower gar-dens when not hidden by snow.

"What a lovely home," Joan breathed. "It looks like part of the landscape, and you can't see any sign of it from the road."

Sarah parked before the entrance and surveyed the walls of irregular granite blocks. Though not old, the house gave the feeling of having settled here comfortably a long time ago.

"Shall we?" She reached for her door handle.

She and Joan got out of the car and walked up the path toward the front entrance. As they approached it, the door swung open and a dark-haired woman of about fifty, dressed in black pants and a red and white sweater, greeted them with a smile.

"Hello. I'm Tara Giles, Ms. Middlefield's personal assistant. Won't you come in? Ms. Middlefield is expecting you."

They walked into a flag-stoned entryway. Framed samplers hung on the walls. As they passed through, Sarah wished she had more time to study them. Some looked very old, and she itched to look more closely at the fine stitches and softly faded threads.

They entered a large, airy living room with windows all across the back wall. Beyond them, the stone wall at the back of the property was visible through the bare limbs of a grove of mature trees. Two bird feeders hung only inches outside the glass.

An elderly woman with short-cropped, iron gray hair rose from one of the upholstered wing chairs. She stood a bit shakily and stared only at Joan.

"Look at you, Joan Elizabeth Franklin! I'd know you anywhere." She held out her arms.

CHAPTER FIFTEEN

Joan dropped her bag and flew across the room into her friend's embrace.

"Alice! I knew it had to be you."

The gray-haired woman laughed. "Yes, it's me. But it's been years since anyone's called me Alice." She looked toward Sarah and appraised her. "And you must be Sarah Hart. Welcome."

Sarah stood still in shock for a moment before she could step forward and take Alice's hand. "Thank you. I'm delighted to meet you, and so glad that Joan is able to see you again."

"I was on pins and needles, wondering if it could possibly be you," Joan said. "We tried not to believe, because we didn't want to be crushed if it wasn't."

Alice lifted a hand and grimaced. "I'm sorry. I should have let Karen tell you. But I wanted to leave things open so that I could cancel up until the last minute if I decided I couldn't go through with it. That was foolish. I should have contacted you much sooner, my dear. I don't know what I was afraid of." She patted Joan's hand. "Come sit down and tell me everything."

"Oh dear," Joan said. "That would take some time."

Joan was up to the task, Sarah decided. She retrieved the fallen tote bag and sat down across from the two older women, who settled in on a chintz-covered sofa near the windows.

Alice spoke first. "I suppose you want to tear into me for not keeping in touch, and I wouldn't blame you."

"No, but I am curious." Joan waited, smiling wistfully.

Alice dashed away a tear. "My, oh my." She fumbled in her pocket and brought out a white handkerchief. "How can I explain? It's inexcusable, really. But I thought ... " She gazed pleadingly at Joan. "I'd had so much pain. I thought seeing any of the old crowd again would just bring more sorrow. But I was wrong. I'm happier today than I've felt in a long time. Thank you for coming." She glanced at Sarah. "Thank you for persisting."

"I was glad to do it," Sarah said.

"Yes, I expect you were. You look like a woman who keeps at a task until it's done." Alice chuckled. "I have to admit, I almost said no. But then you sent that picture of me and Joan and my old Chevy. How could I refuse?"

"I hope this meeting isn't painful for you." Joan eyed her anxiously.

"Much less so than I imagined. But Vern." Alice threw Sarah a reproachful look. "I wasn't ready for that. Joan I felt I could handle. But not Vern."

Sarah didn't know whether to apologize or defend Vern, so she said nothing.

"Do you keep in contact with him?" Alice asked Joan.

"No. I'd no idea he was still living, or that he lived only a few hours away. Sarah's the one who told me, just a couple of weeks ago."

They both looked at Sarah, and she cleared her throat. "Vern is the one who started this, actually. He told me he wished he could find you, and one of the people he remembered from school was Joan. Joan and Bob Willis."

"Oh, Bob was such a nice fellow," Alice said.

"Yes, so I've been told." Sarah hesitated. "I learned he passed away a few years ago."

"I read it in the paper," Alice said. "I don't go out too much, but I have kept up with the news since I moved back here."

"When she couldn't get any information from the Willises, she tracked me down," Joan said. "I'm so glad she did. Sarah and I have become good friends. I said to Donald the other night, even if we don't find Alice, I'll treasure Sarah's friendship."

"Thank you," Sarah murmured.

Alice's eyes lit up. "You and Donald are still together then. I'm glad."

"Yes, of course," Joan said. "We're a couple of old fuddy-duddies, but we've had a good time together. We've got three lovely children, too, and four grandchildren. Oh, Alice, I wish you'd been here to see them grow up."

"I wish I had too. But you know, my little Eleanor ..."

"Yes, dear. Sarah found a newspaper account of the accident and told me. I'm so very sorry." Joan slipped her arm about Alice's shoulders.

"Thank you." Alice sniffed and applied her handkerchief. "That's her picture, up there." She gestured toward the mantel.

Sarah stood and walked closer. The portrait of the laughing little girl made her heart ache. She looked over at Alice. "May I bring it over?"

"Of course," Alice said.

Joan took the framed photograph from Sarah and looked down at it for a long moment. "She was beautiful, Alice. I've kept the two pictures of her you sent me when she was a baby. Such a little darling."

"Yes. We were blessed to have her." Alice wiped her eyes again and lifted her other hand. "Let's not be sad now. You know, I retreated from life for a while after I lost Russell and Eleanor, but I can see now what a mistake that was. Ah!" She looked up as Tara entered the room with a laden tray.

"I thought you ladies might be ready for some refreshments." Tara set the tray on the broad pine coffee table.

Sarah stood. "May I pour the tea for us?"

"Oh, certainly." Alice rubbed her hands together. "I'm getting arthritic, and it's hard for me to hold a heavy teapot steady."

"I have the same problem," Joan said. "In fact, when I was reading your book *Before the Storm*, it was so thick I had trouble holding it."

Alice smiled ruefully. "I've taken to writing thinner ones now. That one was the book of my heart, and I'm afraid I threw in just about everything."

Joan laughed. "Everything from the soda shop to the necklace I gave you."

"Ah, so you noticed that."

"Yes, and I could kick myself for not reading that book years ago, when it was first published. I'd have hunted you down, if I'd known where to look."

"I was still in Colorado when it came out, but then I moved up to Montana. Hiding out, I was. I wanted to keep away from everyone who knew me."

Sarah poured a cup of tea. "Here you are, Joan. Would you like me to put cream or sugar in? We've lemons, too, I see."

"Just like this is fine, thank you," Joan said.

"I like a couple of lemons on the side with mine, please," Alice told Sarah.

Soon they all sat back with their teacups, and Tara came in with sugar cookies and cream cheese brownies.

"Mrs. Hart, tell me about yourself," Alice said.

"Well, I've lived in Maple Hill my whole life. I restore antique quilts and make a few new ones. It's a hobby that became a business, and it's helped me pass the time since my husband passed away. I also let two rooms to boarders, though one is empty right now."

"How interesting. I'm afraid I could never put up with boarders, though to be fair, Tara lives at the other end of the house from me, and we get along well."

Tara smiled and nodded to her employer as she set down the cookie plate. "We're blessed with compatible personalities. Is there anything else I can get you?"

"I believe we're all set. Thank you." When Tara had left the room, Alice continued in a conspiratorial tone. "She does everything for me. Everything. That one's a gem. If I ever lose her, I'll be sunk."

"If you don't mind my asking," Sarah said, "I'd love to know how you became a novelist. Joan didn't think you did much creative writing as a girl. She had no idea that you were writing a novel after you and Russell were married."

Joan set her cup down. "I was surprised, but the more I think it over, the more I realize how fitting it is. You were always so clever, Alice, and I believed you could do anything you set your mind to. I can't believe I didn't find out sooner, though."

"Ah, yes." Alice sighed and sipped her tea. "I suppose there's no getting out of it, so I'll tell you. Russell encouraged me to write. He saw the journal I'd written for the baby, while

I was expecting. It was something new for me, a diversion during my pregnancy. I'd put down a lot of things about my own childhood and the family—Concord and school and you, Joan."

"That's a bit frightening."

Alice laughed. "No, don't feel that way. I wanted my daughter to know what I'd been like when I was young." Sadness swept over her face again, and she put her cup to her lips.

Alice took a swallow and set her cup and saucer down, seeming to have recovered her poise. "It took me a long time to put it in the shape I wanted, but Russell kept telling me to send it off to some publisher or other. I didn't tell anyone what I was doing—not even you, Joan. I submitted that first book under a pen name. I wasn't sure I wanted my acquaintances to know I'd written it if it got into print and earned terrible reviews."

They all chuckled.

"But why Marjory Middlefield?" Joan asked.

Alice shrugged. "Does Alice Farmer sound like a romance author to you?"

"Marjory Middlefield does have a romantic cadence to it," Sarah said.

"Why, thank you." Alice inhaled deeply and held one hand out, palm up. "I sent it off, and I didn't hear for months. Now I realize that's normal, but at the time I was quite on edge about it. After four or five months, Russell said I should write to the editor and ask about it, but I was too timid. Then he told me to send it to someone else, but I wasn't sure that was ethical. So I did nothing. Then..." She pressed her lips tightly together for a moment. "Then we had the accident."

"You were in the car, weren't you?" Sarah asked gently.

Alice let out a big sigh and nodded. "Yes. I was quite banged up, and they didn't want to tell me at first that Russell and Eleanor were both gone. When I found out, I was inconsolable. I had to have a home nurse during my recovery, and it was both long and painful. For months I didn't want to see anyone but my mother."

A lump formed in Sarah's throat. Joan fumbled for a tissue.

"I didn't write to anyone," Alice said. "I didn't even write in my journal. It was just too hard."

Joan wiped her eyes. "So difficult."

"Yes. I got your letters, but I couldn't read them. They'd send me off crying again. Mother put them aside, but I never answered them. Poor Joan. I'm sorry I treated you so badly. But years later, when I'd recovered more or less, I was too ashamed to write to you."

"Oh, my dear. I'm sorry you felt that way."

Tears welled in Sarah's eyes as the two old women embraced.

"What brought you out of that awful time?" Joan asked as she sat back, dabbing her eyes with her tissue.

"Need and my publisher. The funeral expenses and my medical bills took most of Russell's insurance. I had to earn a living, but I dreaded going out and finding a job. Then the editor wrote and said they wanted to buy my book. I was shocked. The advance gave me hope and an excuse to stay in seclusion for several more months."

"The book did well?" Joan asked.

"Yes, moderately. It didn't make any best-seller lists. But it did all right, and the publisher wanted more. They offered me a larger advance for the next book. I saw it as the answer to seeing to my physical needs, though emotionally I was still a wreck."

"Of course," Joan said.

Alice shrugged and reached for another cookie. "Suddenly I had money. I could do whatever I wanted. But I no longer wanted to do anything. Not without Russell and Eleanor. So I bought a house in Montana. Mother and I moved up there. I stayed at home and wrote books. I buried myself in the Middle Ages. I daresay you think that odd, but it was a romantic time period that distracted me from my present-day sorrow."

Joan shook her head, her eyes shining in admiration. "I'm going to read every one of your books."

"Don't torture yourself—if you like that sort of thing, it's all right. Some people find them deadly." Alice lifted her cup and took a sip.

"Let me freshen that for you." Sarah sat forward and refilled their cups.

"So I got back into writing," Alice said. "I holed up in a hundred-year-old house in Montana. My books and the research for them became my passion. Then Mother died in 1978. I was horribly alone then. By this time I needed help with reader mail and so forth. I found Tara. She was young, but diligent and willing to adapt to my idiosyncrasies. I kept writing."

Joan's face was troubled, and Sarah wondered if they were having the same thoughts—that Alice had missed out on so much love and friendship during that time of seclusion. Right after Gerry's death, she'd felt swallowed up in pain. She didn't know how she could have made it through without the friends and family who supported her, surrounding her with their unconditional love.

Alice smiled at them. "About ten years ago I decided to move back to Massachusetts. I realized that I wanted to go home. I'd always thought I'd have children and grandchildren to love me in my old age, but I had no one but Tara. She agreed to come with me, and I bought this lovely, secluded house. It was near town and medical care but isolated enough so that I didn't have to meet people. I found a good housekeeper. I hardly ever leave home, which suits me." She looked over at Sarah. "Tara's started seeing a young widower from church. She insists she'll stay nearby if she gets married and keep working for me days, but...well, no matter how hard we try to avoid it, things change."

"Yes, they do," Joan said.

Alice looked over at Sarah. "All right, I admit I'm curious. Tell me, Sarah. Why does Vern think he wants to see me after all this time?"

"Well, I can't speak for him," Sarah said. "But he told me how much he regrets not keeping in contact with you. And he said he needs to give you a message that's very important."

"So he'd like to ease his conscience before he dies."

Sarah frowned. "Maybe. But I got the impression he was truly repentant and felt he'd wronged you."

"So he did, but there's nothing he can do to fix that now."

"Perhaps not." Sarah watched Alice. Her hostess's wrinkled face held a wistful air, yet Sarah sensed she wasn't ready to grant an easy forgiveness.

Joan leaned toward Alice. "Perhaps he has something particular to tell you, my dear. Shouldn't he have that chance?"

Alice pursed her lips and looked at Sarah again. "How did he bring it up?"

"Wanting to find you? I saw your picture. It was an accident, really." Sarah opened her purse and took out her little notebook. Tucked inside was the photo Vern had given her. "This fell out of his pocket, and I picked it up for him. It was the first time I knew of your existence. He seemed embarrassed at first. But I told him and his grandson that I ..." She felt her cheeks flush as she struggled for the right words. "I've helped a few people ... unravel puzzles in their lives. Vern wanted to find you ... or at least to learn what had happened to you since 1941, and whether or not you were still alive."

"Hmm." Alice took the picture and stared down at it. "My senior picture." She turned it over. A faint smile curved the corners of her lips as she looked at the inscription. "Yes, I gave it to him. It was quite daring of me, when Daddy was so staunchly against Vern."

Sarah took out another photo—one she'd snapped of Vern at Bradford Manor. "Would you like to see what he looks like now?"

Alice reached for it. "Yes, I suppose so." She took it and looked down at it for several seconds. "He's changed."

"You didn't expect him to look eighteen, did you?" Joan asked with a laugh. "Let me see."

Alice handed over the picture. Joan frowned down at it. "Well, it's been nearly seventy years, after all. He used to be quite good looking, though."

"He'd like to see you again." Sarah held her breath.

Alice nodded slowly. "All right. Why not? I'll go up to Maple Hill with you to meet him," Alice said. "I've stayed holed up too long. My agent comes to me here once in a while, but I do almost all my business over the telephone or by e-mail nowadays. But Tara drives me places when I need to go. Maybe she'd take me to Maple Hill." Alice reached for Joan's hand. "I'm so sorry now that I cut myself off so decidedly. I can see that we might have had some good times together, Joan."

Joan smiled, her eyes glistening. "Yes, we might have. But we still can, my dear. I don't intend to let you shut me out of your life again. And you don't have to keep Vern in it if you don't want. But it might be just as well to see him once. Perhaps his regrets are as strong as yours."

Sarah took back the picture Alice handed her. "I think he's wished for years he had a chance to speak to you, and perhaps to explain his actions. But it never came about easily, so he let it go. And now he feels time is short. As Joan said, it need only be a brief meeting, if that's all you want. But it might make a big difference to him and how he faces the rest of his life."

Alice eyed her speculatively. "He was married, wasn't he? I've wondered, you know, but you said he has a grandson."

"Yes, he was. He had a son, but I believe he's gone now. I've met his grandson Scott, who is married and has a child. Scott told me he and the little boy are Vern's only living descendants."

"Well, I'd say that's sad, but it's more than I've got. I hope he had some happy years."

"I'm sure he did," Sarah said.

"I did wonder if he'd met another girl. Maybe one of his nurses while he was in the hospital."

"You know, I don't know how he met his wife." Sarah realized she'd never asked Vern much about his life outside of his high school and army days. There was still a great deal she didn't know about him.

Tara reentered the room carrying a different teapot on a tray. "I thought you ladies might like a fresh pot of tea."

"Tara," Alice said, "I want to take a trip."

"Oh?" Tara stopped and looked down at her. "Are you sure?"

"Yes. I want to go to Maple Hill. I've an old friend there who can't come to me, so I must go to him."

"All right. Perhaps in the spring?"

"No, no." Alice raised herself up from the sofa. "I want to go soon. Not today, but Saturday, perhaps. I'm not getting any younger, and neither is Vern Pickett."

Sarah chimed in. "I'd be happy to host you at my house. Vern fell a month or so ago and is in a rehabilitation facility so he can receive physical therapy for the leg he injured. Perhaps you would be more comfortable meeting each other at my home."

"That sounds wise," Tara said. "We could take Mrs. Nash with us if she's willing."

"I'd love to go," Joan assured her.

"Well..." Alice looked to Sarah.

Sarah nodded. "I think it's a good plan too. And I was thinking...I have an empty guest room. If you wanted to, you could stay over in Maple Hill, at my home. That way, you wouldn't have to drive so far in one day. My son and his wife have a huge house in town, and I'm sure I could arrange for them to put up Joan and Tara if you decided to stay over."

"Oh no, I couldn't do that," Alice said. She sank down onto the sofa, and Joan sat beside her.

"No one would know who you were," Joan said. "And we'll call you Alice, so no one would know the famous Marjory Middlefield had come to town."

Alice exhaled heavily. "Let's not talk about that. Today I am Alice again, and do you know what?" The old twinkle was back in her eyes as she looked at Joan. "I want to be Alice."

"So this weekend, then?" Sarah asked.

"Monday might be better," Tara said, looking anxiously at Alice.

"That's right, you have plans for Saturday. I forgot."

Tara's face tinged with pink. "Perhaps I could reschedule."

"No, there's no need for that." Alice turned to Sarah. "Would Monday suit you?"

"It's fine," Sarah said.

"Oh, dear. When is my next deadline? I'll be too excited to write this weekend." Alice rubbed her hands together in her lap.

Tara answered. "It's not until the end of February, and you said last night that the next book is nearly done."

"Yes, so it is." Alice's shoulders relaxed and she turned eagerly to Joan and Sarah. "It takes place in France in the fourteenth century. Fascinating period!" Her sharp gaze darted to Tara again. "Oh! You must fetch copies of the last book. Has either of you read *The Celtic Courtship?*"

Tara brought the books and a pen, and Alice began to inscribe them. Sarah hesitated and decided to bring up Vanessa. "The friend who lent me your book is an avid fan of yours. Would you mind if I brought another book for you to sign for her? I know you don't go out and do book signings, but it would mean a great deal to her."

Alice's eyes lit. "I can do better than that. I'll sign one for her right now." She looked up at her assistant. "Could you bring another book for me, Tara?"

"Certainly. Is there one your friend hasn't read?"

"I'm sure there isn't," Sarah said. "She says she has every book Marjory Middlefield's ever written."

"Oh, I know." Alice looked eagerly up at Tara. "Remember the script for the film they made from *The Marcher Lord's Lady*? Didn't we have two of those? I'll bet an avid fan would love to have a signed copy of the movie script."

Sarah caught her breath. "Oh, are you sure? That must be a treasure."

Alice shrugged. "I have two, and they're not doing me any good sitting in the supply closet."

"Let her do it," Tara said. "I haven't seen Marjory so excited about her fans in a long time."

Alice sighed and sat back on the sofa. "Yes, she's right. I've been remiss at not connecting with my readers more. Karen Zilt has told me so several times, but I've ignored her. Tara's answered the reader mail, but I haven't...*engaged*. Oh, ladies..." She looked at Joan and then at Sarah with a sweet smile. "I'm so glad you found me."

CHAPTER SIXTEEN

The next morning, Sarah drove to Bradford Manor eager to tell Vern her news. She was a bit tired from her long day, but nothing would keep her from seeing him as soon as possible.

She found him in the lounge, talking to some friends. Sarah greeted them all, then turned to Vern.

"I have some news for you."

"Good news, I hope?"

"Very good."

He grinned. "I was just about to head back to my room."

She followed him down the hallway. In his room, he turned his wheelchair to face the recliner and nodded for Sarah to sit there. Before she'd sat down, he said, "It's about Alice?"

"Yes. She's alive."

He exhaled and closed his eyes for a moment. "Thank you, Sarah."

"I saw her yesterday. Joan and I went to her home in Lexington."

He sat still for a moment, and Sarah waited, not wanting to rush things.

"How is she?" he asked at last.

"She's doing well physically. I thought she was quite spry for her age, especially since she rarely goes out, and she spends a lot of time sitting and writing. But she told us that she exercises every day." Sarah smiled. "She has a weight machine. Can you believe that?"

Vern nodded. "Yeah, I can. But I'm surprised she doesn't go out. Alice was always the life of the party in high school."

"The tragedy in her life changed her, Vern. She lost her husband and her little girl in a car accident in 1951. She had a hard time dealing with her grief, but she's much better now."

"I'm sorry she went through all that." He arched his eyebrows. "So . . . what did Alice say about me? Was she mad at me?"

"You really think she'd be angry after all this time?"

Vern shrugged. "I guess I would be. But Alice . . . maybe not."

"Well, she wasn't angry, but she did express some hurt about the way you disappeared from her life. You meant a lot to her."

He nodded, but said nothing.

"She'd planned on marrying you, Vern."

"Yeah," he whispered. "I really messed up."

"And then, when she'd finally moved on and met someone else, it looked like she might have a happy life, after all. But then her husband and her little girl died. And after a few more years, she lost her mother too. She's felt very alone in her adulthood."

Tears glistened in Vern's eyes.

She smiled gently. "But she seemed happy yesterday. Happy that we'd nudged her to break the silence. I'm positive that she was glad to see Joan again, so you can be thankful for that. If you hadn't started me looking for Alice, she and Joan probably never would have seen each other again."

"That's good. I'm glad something positive came out of it."

"And she wanted to know what you'd been up to and how your health was," Sarah said. "She did ask if you had a family."

"Huh." He pressed his lips together. "Did you tell her?"

"Yes. I took a few pictures on my cell phone, if you're interested in seeing what she looks like now."

"Sure."

Sarah took out her phone and brought up the best picture she'd taken the day before. "This is Alice." She handed it over to him.

Vern gazed at the small screen for a long time. "She's still beautiful."

"Yes, she is." Sarah reached for the phone. "There's another picture of her and Joan that's really cute. They were like kids again, hugging and talking nineteen to the dozen." She handed the phone back with the second photo showing.

"Ha. That is nice." He gave the phone back.

"Oh, and here's the one you lent me that first day." Sarah took the small photograph of Alice from her notebook and handed it to him.

Vern glanced at it and tucked it into his pocket. "Will I— will I get a chance to meet her?"

"She'd like to see you."

His gray eyebrows shot up. "She would?"

"Yes. She's going to try to get over here on Monday. To my house, that is. She has someone to drive her and Joan over. I'll see if Scott or my son can take you to my house that day, if you're willing."

"Monday?" It came out almost a croak.

"Yes. Is that all right? We could put it off a few days if you'd like."

"No, that's okay." He huffed out a breath.

"Vern?"

"Yeah?"

Sarah eyed him closely. "You did say you wanted to find her. I mean...that's what you wanted, isn't it?"

"Well, yeah." He frowned and stared down at the rug for a moment, then gave a quick shrug. "Sure. Monday's good. I mean, we've waited long enough, right?"

Sarah wondered if she'd made a huge mistake. Was it possible Vern wanted to know that Alice was still alive, but didn't really want to see her at all?

Sarah drove to church with Belle beside her Sunday morning, driving slowly through snowy streets. Six inches of new powder had fallen in the night, and the plows were still cleaning up the aftermath.

As they passed the pastor's house, she saw her son's vehicle parked at the curb.

Belle said, "There's Jason."

Sarah glanced over. Jason was working his way toward John's front steps, wielding a shovel to carve a path. The steps were completely blanketed in snow. "Oh boy. Looks like we forgot to assign that job."

At the church, they found Martha in the entry, wringing her hands and peering out the window in the door. "Hello, Sarah. Belle. Do you know if Jason's over at the pastor's house yet?"

"He was there when we came by," Sarah said.

Martha shook her head, frowning. "I don't know how I overlooked the shoveling. I knew Jason would pick him up, and I guess I assumed one of the trustees would shovel John's walk. But when we drove by this morning, the driveway hadn't been touched, and I called Jason right away. They'll probably be late for the service."

"Let's see if someone else can go and help him," Sarah said.

"I'll help." Belle handed Sarah her Bible. "Is there another shovel here?"

Sarah strode to the closet just inside the double doors. "Here you go, Belle. We'll see if we can round up some more help."

Twenty minutes later, Belle was back.

"All set," she whispered.

Moments later, Sarah heard voices and stamping feet in the entry. The pastor rolled into the narthex with Jason guiding his wheelchair and two other men, who had belatedly gone to help Jason, behind them.

When it was time for the worship service, Pastor John stood behind the pulpit leaning on his crutches.

"Folks, it's wonderful to be back."

Everyone clapped.

He smiled, and when the applause died down, he went on, "Last week was good, but this is better. I'm not going to stand up here the whole time, but I wanted to remind myself of what it feels like to be in this spot. And I want to say thank you for the love you've shown me over the past few weeks."

He looked out over the congregation and nodded slowly. "This church is a wonderful group of people. I know several of you gave up large chunks of your time to help me out. Friends, I don't think I've eaten so well since I left home for college more than thirty years ago."

A ripple of laughter ran through the congregation.

Pastor John's face went sober as he continued. "There's one person I want to give special thanks to. She's spent hours and hours this month making sure I'd be comfortable and well fed. She chased some of you down and got you to tend to things I normally would have done myself. And if you couldn't do it, she did it herself."

Ernie elbowed his wife. Sitting beside Martha, Sarah smiled at her. Martha ducked her head, and her cheeks flushed a lovely pink.

Heads began to swivel, and Pastor John nodded. "You got it. You all know who I'm talking about. Martha, you've shown the love of Christ in your efforts this month. Thank you so much."

Martha sniffed and gave him a quick little wave.

"And Ernie," Pastor John said, smiling down at him, "I don't think you'll mind, will you, if I give Martha a big hug after the service?"

"Hug away, Pastor," Ernie said.

Sarah opened her purse and pulled out a tissue for Martha.

Pastor John nodded. "Great. Now, I know there were a lot of jobs that people jumped in to help with, besides cooking for me. Oh, by the way, you ladies can stop the meals now. It's been wonderful, but it's time I fend for myself again."

A ripple ran through the crowd. Martha sighed deeply.

"Most of the jobs you folks took over probably got done better than I could have done them. In fact, this morning some of you took on a job I had no idea needed to be done. The fellow who plows me out apparently had me last on his list today. Thanks to those of you who pitched in."

"Amen," Harry Butler called.

At the end of the service, Pastor John dismissed the people and came down off the platform, assisted by Harry. On his crutches, he swung over to stand in the aisle by the Maplethorpes.

"You came for your hug, didn't you?" Martha gave him a squeeze.

Pastor John chuckled. "Martha, was there anything else left that didn't get done? Because as far as I know, things have gone like clockwork here."

Martha's mouth twitched. "There's only one thing I can think of. We still need somebody to drive to Logan International for the missionary speaker on Friday. He needs to be picked up at three o'clock."

Harry Butler said, "You've been working on that for quite a while. We'd better settle it right now."

"Now, Harry—" Pastor John's words were drowned as Harry raised his voice.

"Folks, we need somebody to step up and commit to picking up the missionary in Boston on Friday."

A hush fell over the crowd of people exiting the sanctuary. Pastor John looked over the congregation. Most of the men looked elsewhere. Sarah started to open her mouth, but Martha jabbed her with her elbow.

"I had planned to pick up Mr. Raines myself," John said. "He's an old friend of mine. But the doctor says I can't drive for at least two more weeks. If anyone is able, I'd be happy to ride along."

Slowly, Nathan Shoop stepped forward. "I'll go, Pastor."

"Thank you, Nathan."

Nathan nodded. "I know Martha's asked me two or three times to do stuff, but I couldn't get away. Guess the world won't end if I shut the store early on Friday and drive over to Boston."

Martha caught Sarah's eye and winked.

Jason cleared his throat, where he stood near Maggie. He looked around at all the people. "Maggie and I haven't lived here long, but we've seen the work Martha's been doing. The people here have come together to get through a tough time for the church. I don't know about you, but I've learned some things from it. For one thing, people have got to help each other, even when it hurts. But also, I learned how much you've been doing, Pastor John, besides studying and preaching."

"He's been doing too much," Ernie said.

Jason nodded. "If we all kept doing some of these jobs we've been asked to do during this time, we could probably cover most of the little things Pastor John's been doing outside his job description."

Several people murmured, "That's right."

Pastor John looked around, and his gaze came back to Jason. "I'm touched by what you're saying. But I don't want—"

Ernie held up his hand. "We know, John. You don't want to put anyone out. Let us pick up the slack, like we've mostly done this month. It hasn't hurt us, and it will give you more time to spend on your real job."

"Amen," said Harry Butler.

"And I know just the woman to hand out the assignments." Ernie smiled and everyone chuckled.

Sarah leaned toward Martha. "You really have done a super job. Are you up to more charts and schedules?"

"I think so." Martha smiled as Angela Miller came to her and reached to hug her.

"Thank you for all you've done, Martha. You can put me down for a job."

"I'll call you," Martha promised.

Sarah stood back as several other people came over to thank Martha. It warmed her heart to see so many tell her friend how much they appreciated her efforts. Pastor John made his way to the door to speak to people on the way out, but the people lingered to talk, and the crowd thinned slowly.

Another inch of fresh snow fell during the night Sunday, but the weatherman promised Monday would be clear. Sarah woke early. She tried to go back to sleep, but her nerves wouldn't let her. Today Alice would finally meet Vern.

Would their reunion go smoothly, or was disaster awaiting them? Sarah thought about what she had learned about Alice and Vern. Vern's forgetfulness still bothered her, but she had filled in some of the gaps through her research. She had spent hours pondering the discrepancies she'd found, and the sketchy information he had given her about his family. The picture of him in uniform kept niggling at her mind too. Was she making a huge mistake?

She calmed herself and prayed for God's blessing on the reunion. Finally she rose, knowing her guests wouldn't arrive until eleven o'clock or later.

Belle had helped her clean the house thoroughly, and Sarah had made two fruit pies. As usual she had over-prepared, but she knew she'd fret less if she had too much food on hand.

She laid out the dishes and fussed about in the kitchen. After seasoning the chicken, she put it back in the refrigerator and made herself eat breakfast. Belle came down and opened the refrigerator.

"Are you nervous this morning?"

"Why do you ask?" Sarah arched her eyebrows at Belle's back.

Belle turned around grinning and holding up Sarah's cell phone. "Expecting a cold call?"

"Oh! Really?" Sarah stood and took it from her. The phone felt icy in her hand. "How did I do that?"

"Better check your purse and see if you put a stick of butter in there."

Sarah waved a hand at her, chuckling at Belle's teasing. "I do hope they have a safe trip over."

"So do I."

After Belle left for work, Sarah sat down at her computer. She had driven to Scott and McKenna's house on Sunday afternoon and borrowed the picture of Vern in his uniform. Now she took it and laid it beside the computer. The two young men stood tall and straight—Vern's friend several inches taller than Vern himself. His expressive dark eyes glinted at the camera. Even now, Vern's eyes held that same determined look. The other soldier had lighter eyes, and he, too, looked ready to take on the world.

Sarah focused on the dark spot on Vern's side of the picture. Was it a stain of some kind? She turned the frame over to see if she could remove the picture easily without damaging it. Better not try without asking Scott, she decided, but she wished that part of the photo was clear.

The retired sergeant in charge of the squadron's reunion had directed her to a site dedicated to the Massachusetts 182nd National Guard unit. She had viewed it on Saturday, but she wanted to browse the photos again. Reaching for the mouse, she clicked on her Web browser, then the site she had bookmarked.

The ringing of her cell phone startled her.

"It's Tara, Mrs. Hart."

"Hello, Tara. Please call me Sarah."

"All right. I just wanted you to know that we're on schedule. We've stopped to stretch our legs and expect to arrive just about eleven."

"Thank you for letting me know. Is everyone traveling well?"

"Yes, indeed. The ladies are enjoying the drive and each other's company."

"I'm so glad," Sarah said. "I'll see you soon."

She turned back to the Web site and clicked on a tab that said "Photo Album." Black-and-white pictures flickered across the screen. One was labeled, "182nd preparing to leave for New Caledonia, July 1942." It seemed odd that their uniforms were a solid drab color, not the camouflage so common nowadays.

Sarah scanned the faces. At least thirty uniformed men were caught by the camera as they formed up, their gear piled nearby. She squinted at the fine print at the bottom of the screen. A list of last names ran beneath the photo, though she didn't need it to be certain about who she was looking at. "Avery, Nelson, Reynolds, Johnson, Pickett." She held the snapshot up next to the screen. In both pictures, he looked very young and handsome, but a little anxious. His friend was not in the on-screen photo. Sarah wished she knew his name. She zoomed in on the nearest soldier's sleeve patch for the 182nd. Very distinctive insignia. She picked up her cell phone and opened the photo she'd snapped of Vern at Bradford Manor.

"The eyes say it all," she murmured, holding it up to Scott's framed picture.

Though Sarah had begun this quest looking for Alice Ward, now she found herself searching just as hard for Vern Pickett and the past that had shaped him into what he was today. She shook her head. Today would be very interesting.

Jason drove in first. Sarah grabbed her jacket and pulled it on. January temperatures ruled, though the sun shone brightly.

She hurried out and opened the passenger door of the vehicle to greet Vern.

"Hi, Vern! Welcome."

"Thanks. Glad to be here." He stood and leaned on his cane.

"No wheelchair?" Sarah asked.

"I graduated to a walking stick."

"That's good news."

With Sarah on one side of him and Jason on the other, they walked toward the house.

"Would the back door be easier?" Jason asked.

Sarah glanced toward the steps leading up to the wraparound porch and the front door. "Probably. There are fewer steps out back."

"Let's do that." Jason guided Vern toward the path that led around the house.

Inside her kitchen, Sarah took his coat and hat.

Vern took off his fogged-up glasses and rubbed the lenses on his sleeve. "Thank you for bringing me, young man."

"You're welcome," Jason said.

Sarah smiled at her son. "Yes, thank you, Jason.

"No problem. I've got a meeting scheduled with a client, though, so I've got to get back to my office."

Sarah hated to see him drive off, but she was glad his business had picked up a little.

She led Vern into the living room and settled him in a comfortable chair near the fireplace.

"Oh, you have a fire." He leaned eagerly toward it. "It's been a long time since I got to sit by one like this."

Sarah smiled. "I love it on a cold winter day. Enjoy it while we wait for the others. Can I bring you something to drink?"

She ran through a list of beverages, and Vern decided on hot chocolate. When she'd placed the mug and a dish of marshmallows on the end table near him, he asked, "Who else is coming?"

"Just Alice and Joan and Alice's assistant, who's driving them. You and Alice can have some time to talk privately if you want."

He nodded soberly. "I appreciate that."

Sarah went over to the end table, where she'd left the borrowed picture. "Vern, I wanted to ask you about this."

He stared at the framed photo in her hand, then looked up at her. "Where did you get that?"

"From Scott. He lent it to me. I found your regiment's Web site, and there was a photo of your platoon getting ready to ship out for New Caledonia."

"Really?"

"Yes. I wanted to see if I could locate you and your friend in the picture." She paused. "I know the truth."

Vern opened his mouth and closed it. "So now what?"

"Are you going to tell everyone the truth?"

He nodded. "I am."

Sarah heard another car drive in and peeked out the window. She turned back to Vern.

"They're here. Are you sure you want to do this?" At Vern's nod, Sarah stood. "Just stay where you are, and I'll bring the ladies in." Her heart pounding, she hurried out to the garage entry.

Tara was getting out of the car when Sarah reached it. She went to the passenger side.

"If you'd like to give Joan a hand, I'll help Marjory," Tara called. "That is, Alice." She smiled and shook her head. "I'm still getting used to this."

"Hello, Joan, dear," Sarah said as she opened the rear door and found Joan smiling out at her. "I hope you had a good journey."

"Yes, it was marvelous. We gabbed the whole way."

"Is Vern here?" Alice's voice quavered as she stood and looked at Sarah's Queen Anne house.

"Yes, he's inside waiting for us," Sarah said. "My son brought him over."

"Oh, will we meet your son?" Joan asked.

"Probably not today."

Sarah guided Joan around to the back door, and Tara followed with Alice.

"What a lovely home you have," Alice said as she walked in and looked around the kitchen.

"Thank you." Sarah took their wraps and hung them in the hall closet. Alice wore navy blue pants and a blue and white striped sweater, while Joan had chosen a red print skirt with a red blouse and black jacket.

"You both look lovely," Sarah said.

"Thank you," Joan replied, but Alice was looking about nervously, her jaw working slightly as she took it in.

Sarah smiled. "All right, ladies, I know you're all anxious to see Vern." She turned toward the living room. Vern struggled to get up from the armchair. Sarah started forward to help him, but he'd managed before she could take two steps and stood leaning on his cane.

Alice entered the room and paused. An indecipherable look crossed her lined face as she gazed at Vern.

He hobbled across the room and stopped, facing Alice. "Well. After all these years." He bent toward her and kissed her gently on the cheek.

Alice's eyebrows arched. She gazed at him intently as he pulled back.

Did she know? Sarah waited for her to speak.

"Hello," Alice said. "You're not Vern, are you?"

CHAPTER SEVENTEEN

Joan gasped. She and Tara edged up beside Sarah, watching Alice and Vern.

After a long pause, Vern said quietly, "No, I'm not." Sarah realized she was holding her breath, waiting to see what would happen next.

Alice cocked her head to one side. "What does this mean, then? Why am I here? Please don't tell me you're my greatest fan and went to all this trouble to meet me in person. You're too old for that sort of nonsense."

"No, no," he said. "I wouldn't do that. I have a message for you. I should have come in '45 and given it to you straight away, but I didn't. And the longer I waited, the harder it got. I'm sorry."

Sarah pulled in a deep breath. "Why don't we all sit down?"

Tara touched Alice's arm. "Marjory, dear, I'm so sorry. I had no idea this was a hoax. Do you want to leave?"

"Please," Sarah said. "I don't think it's a hoax exactly, and I'm sure Vern doesn't mean her any harm." She looked pleadingly to Vern. Her stomach churned as she waited for his assurance.

"I don't," he said. "But I'd like the chance to tell Alice my story. And Vern's."

Alice gazed at him long and hard. Finally she nodded. "Tara, you've done a wonderful job of shielding me from unpleasantness for more than thirty years. But I think this is something I need to see through. If this gentleman and I could have a few minutes..."

"Are you certain?" Tara's eyes narrowed as she appraised Vern.

"All I want to do is talk," he said. "I promise I won't take advantage of Sarah's generous hospitality. She's been a true friend to me." He looked Sarah in the eye. "I regret not being up front with you from the start, but I couldn't. You can be sure I mean no harm."

Sarah tried to see him objectively—an eighty-seven-year-old man who couldn't walk without a cane. She could probably knock him over with one finger.

Tara turned to Sarah. "Did you know he was an impostor?"

"I suspected. There were little things. For instance, Joan telling me that Vern had eyes like Paul Newman—and Paul Newman's eyes were very blue. I found some concrete evidence yesterday, but I wasn't a hundred percent sure until just now."

"I can't believe this entire thing was a charade," Tara said. "How long have you known him?"

"Only a few weeks." Sarah grimaced. "But he didn't come up with the name suddenly, I assure you. His grandson is named Scott Pickett."

"Sarah—" He put out one hand in a gesture of friendship. "Yes?"

"I didn't mean to lie to you. I apologize for that. It's been so long...I haven't really thought of it as lying for many years. Vern Pickett is my name now. I've thought of myself as Vern for almost seventy years."

She nodded. "I'm not sure I understand it all, but I'd like to hear your explanation. I trust you."

"All right, let's get on with it." Alice walked between Sarah and Vern and sat down in Sarah's mission rocking chair. "I'm listening."

Vern took his glasses off and rubbed his eyes, then put them back on. "Ladies, it wasn't my intention to bring you here under false pretenses. I couldn't help thinking that if I didn't take this chance, and if I put it off any longer...well, that I might never have another opportunity.

"I hope I can leave Bradford Manor soon, but they tell me I can't live alone when I do, so I'll be going to live with my grandson Scott and his family." Vern sighed. "Scott doesn't know any of this. I guess there's a lot I'll have to tell him." He shot a glance at Sarah. "Unless you told him?"

"No. I only borrowed the picture from him. I didn't explain why."

He smiled ruefully. "That picture."

Sarah picked it up. "It's you and the real Vern, isn't it?"

"Yes. One of his buddies took it."

"He's wearing the 182nd Massachusetts patch, but you weren't. That's why you inked it out on your uniform. You weren't in Vern's unit at the start, were you?"

"No." Vern shook his head. "You're one smart lady. I wondered if I ought to let you start digging. But it would have ended this way, anyhow. I'd have told Alice the truth once I found her, whether you knew it or not."

"Well, we already know you're not Vern," Joan said. "I should have guessed when I saw the picture Sarah showed us. I just figured you'd changed a lot."

Tara leaned forward. Her gaze drilled into Vern. "The question is, if you're not Vern Pickett, who are you?"

He hiked his chin up. "Richard. Richard Carini." Vern sighed. "A lot of years have gone by since I said that name out loud."

"Carini," Joan said. "That's not a Concord name."

"Never heard of it," said Alice.

"No. No, you girls never heard of me back in 1941, when you knew Vern. Back then, Vern and I didn't know each other existed. That came a couple of years later, when we found ourselves in the same platoon, slogging through the jungle in the Solomons."

Sarah relaxed a little. She'd known, somehow, that it began there—after Vern left Concord. After he'd enlisted. Nearer the time when he stopped writing to Alice, she guessed. She gave him an encouraging smile. "Tell us what happened."

Vern licked his lips and looked down at her red Oriental rug. "I lived in Illinois. Came from a big Italian family."

"I knew it," Alice said. "You don't look at all like the Picketts. Too slight, and your skin's too dark. I'll bet you had darker hair than Vern, too, before you went gray."

Vern nodded. "That's right. My whole family had dark hair and brown eyes. Vern had blue eyes and light hair. Kind of sandy, you might say. He was taller than me, and a little heavier. He was a good-looking guy." He gave a rueful chuckle. "I was always afraid someone who knew him would see me and know... but that comes later. See, I got in some trouble in 1942."

"What kind of trouble?" Tara's voice still had a hard edge. Sarah could tell she hadn't let Vern off the hook yet.

He looked away from Tara's accusing gaze. "I'd got in with the wrong crowd. We did some things...things I regret. The last thing—the one that decided my future—was holding up a corner store." He shook his head. "I'm not making any excuses. It was wrong, and we all knew it. Well, one of my friends—" he chuckled mirthlessly, "took along a gun. See, I thought we were just going to walk into the store and kind of cover for each other while we filched a few things. But this guy had something else in mind. To make a long story short, he shot the owner of the store."

Sarah swallowed hard and darted a glance at Tara. She hadn't expected anything this sordid. Maybe Tara wasn't far off the mark in her protectiveness of Alice.

"I was already halfway out the door when I heard the shot, but I just kept running. I didn't look back."

He was silent a long time. Sarah felt ill as she looked at the others' pale faces.

"Were you arrested?" Joan asked.

Vern shook his head. "But I knew I could be. If any of the others ratted on me, I would be. I didn't dare go home. Later that night I caught up with one of the other kids. He told me Frankie shot the guy in the stomach. And they all ran after I did. One of them had seen a police car headed toward the store. This other kid babbled on about how we might be accessories to murder. That was the worst night of my life."

"What did you do?" Alice asked.

"I headed for the nearest army recruiting station. I was a kid. Only eighteen. I'd thought about enlisting, anyhow, after we got into the war. And that night I only thought about putting distance between me and that store."

"What about your family, Richard?" Alice's voice quivered. "Did you tell them you were going?"

He let out a shaky breath. "I called them after I'd signed the papers the next morning. Talked to my mother. I didn't tell her about the robbery, just that I'd decided to join up. She was upset, but when my pa came on the line, he seemed to think it was a good idea. He always complained about having so many kids to feed." Vern shrugged. "On the other hand, I'd had a part-time job for a while, pumping gas, and I'd been giving half my pay to my mother. I knew she'd miss that. Pa wasn't earning all that much. So I set it up so that my army pay would go to her. She cried when she heard that. I'd like to think she got those checks and that it eased her way a little bit."

Tears stung Sarah's eyes. "I'm sure that was a help to your mother."

Vern nodded, a quick jerk. "Yeah. I felt bad later on about that. After ... " He shook his head. "I guess the checks stopped when I quit being me."

Sarah stood, sensing that they all needed a break. "I was going to fix tea for everyone. Let me do that now."

Tara followed her to the kitchen. "You knew none of this?"

"No." Sarah went to the tray of tea things she'd set out earlier.

"Let me help." Tara followed her instructions efficiently, but she still frowned. "This man—Richard Carini. He's a fraud. He's living under a false name."

"So it seems." Sarah tried to remain serene as she filled the teapot.

Tara shook her head. "I don't know what to make of it."

"Neither do I, yet." Sarah smiled at her. "I do believe what he's told us so far. Let's hear the rest of it before we make up our minds, shall we?"

A few minutes later they all had refreshments and were ready to hear Vern finish his story. He plopped two marsh-mallows into his mug of hot chocolate and glanced at Sarah.

"I guess you gals have figured out that I wound up in the same unit as Vern Pickett."

"It seemed likely to me," Sarah said. "I traced your unit. That is, the Americal Division. Vern's regiment was the 182nd Massachusetts."

"Mine was the 132nd Illinois."

Of course, Sarah thought. "Your units were both sent to New Caledonia and combined with a North Dakota regiment into the Americal."

He nodded. "Some of us who came into it late were replacement troops for men they'd lost. Vern was in it from the start. He'd enlisted right after Pearl Harbor, or maybe even before. I think he told me he joined a couple of weeks before we were officially at war in the Pacific. I joined the Illinois Guard in May of 1942. We shipped out as soon as my basic training was over, and I was glad to be off American soil, fool that I was." He exhaled deeply. "I had no idea what war would be like, but I found out soon enough. The only good thing that happened to me was meeting Vern. He and I got to be friends right away. We had to wait on New Caledonia for weeks, and that's when we got to know each other. I'd have to say, he was like a brother to me."

"I liked him a lot," Joan said. "He could be very charming, right, Alice?"

Alice smiled. "Oh yes. He won my heart without much effort."

"You must have talked to each other a lot," Sarah said, thinking of the things this man knew about the real Vern, and also the things he did not know. Now his "memory lapses" and refusal to talk about certain topics made sense.

"Oh, yeah," he said. "I ended up telling Vern everything that had happened to me—the shooting, all of it. He said if they hadn't come after me by the end of basic training, I was probably all right. He kept reminding me that it wasn't my fault. Vern told me to put the whole mess behind me and do something good with my life. Even when we were up to our knees in swamps, he'd say we were protecting the people back home. People like my family, and like...Alice." He looked over at her. "He talked about you a lot."

"I'm glad he had someone to talk to," Joan said.

Alice nodded. "Me too, but I wouldn't mind knowing exactly what he said about me."

Sarah smiled. So Alice did care, even seventy years later.

Vern's lips curved as though he was remembering a pleasant moment. "Oh, he said plenty. I thought he'd never shut up about Alice. Only thing was, later on, I wished he'd told me more. Wished I'd written it all down too."

"Well?" Alice asked pointedly.

"He said you were the prettiest girl in the school, and the smartest."

"Hm."

Vern's smile broadened. "He told me about you getting all A's and your daddy buying you that car. A 1939 Chevy. Old Vern was downright jealous of that car."

"I let him drive it," Alice said with a guilty shiver.

"Oh yes, he told me that too. Told me you weren't supposed to, but you did, because you liked him a heap."

"Yes, I did. I'd have done just about anything to get his attention. When he started noticing me, I thought I was the luckiest girl in the world."

"The feeling was mutual, believe me. Oh, and he told me about that soda shop you used to go to. Casey's. I never forgot that."

"Alice put it in her first book," Sarah said. "I have a copy for you." Sarah nodded toward the mantelpiece.

"That's ... that's very nice. Thank you." Vern shifted in the chair and looked over at Alice. "Vern did talk a lot about you, especially when we were cooped up in tunnels and trenches for hours and hours with nothing to do. He told me about his family too. That was important. Vern's father was gone, but his mother was still alive. And he had a sister, but they weren't very close."

Sarah's mind spun ahead. The pieces were falling into place quickly.

"Did he tell you about his fight with my father?" Alice asked.

Surprised she'd mentioned it, Sarah sat forward, eager to hear Vern's reply.

"Oh yeah. Said that was what clinched it for him. He'd been thinking of enlisting, but when that happened, he couldn't see sticking around Concord anymore. Your father told him not to come near you again. When I met him, it had been almost a year, but he was still smarting from it."

"Yes," Alice said. "My father was a harsh man in some ways, though he loved me. He didn't want a boy like Vern—that is, a poor boy who would sneak around behind his back—to be in contact with his daughter. He forbade me to see Vern again, or to speak to him on the telephone, or to write him notes. I wondered how that would work out at school, but Vern never came back to school. I never saw him again." She dabbed at her eyes with a tissue.

"I'm very sorry about that. When Sarah started asking me about your father, I was afraid she'd be suspicious, because Vern didn't tell me the exact words the old man said to him, so I couldn't answer Sarah's questions about that. I just knew it went deep with Vern. But by the time I met him, he figured he'd done the right thing to leave. He wanted to come back after the war and go to your father with a different attitude. By then you'd both be older, and he figured Mr. Ward would have to admit Vern had done the honorable thing by respecting his wishes and not seeing you again. Then maybe he'd let Vern court you."

CHAPTER EIGHTEEN

Vern—Richard Carini—took a deep breath. "I suppose I should tell you about what finally happened to the real Vern Pickett.

"We had to wait in New Caledonia for transport. They took the North Dakota boys first. We stayed there with the Massachusetts regiment. We mixed quite a bit, and Vern and I really opened up to each other. We wondered if we'd regret joining the army, but at the same time, we were eager to fight. That's when that picture was taken." He gestured toward the framed snapshot.

"You were wearing the Illinois patch," Sarah said. "Later, you inked over it and told people that was you and your buddy, and no one could tell that you were from different regiments."

He nodded. "It was the only picture I had of the real Vern. I thought about destroying it many times, but I couldn't bring myself to do that." He was quiet for a minute. "We went to Guadalcanal on the same ship. We didn't expect heavy losses. It was more or less a cleanup operation by then." Vern shook his head. "There were still pockets of heavy resistance, though. My squad got separated from the main unit, and the Japanese pinned us down. I'll spare you the bloody details, but half a dozen men from Vern's outfit wound up near us. We took a grenade, and everyone in my unit was killed or badly wounded. The enemy picked off the rest of us. I got hit before Vern did." He sniffed and swiped at his eyes with his cuff. Alice handed him a tissue.

"Take your time, Richard," she said.

He took off his glasses and wiped his eyes then put them back on and inhaled slowly. "Things had gotten really bad. Vern was trying to help me, and there was one other guy from his platoon. They stuck with those of us who were wounded. We started thinking maybe none of us would make it out alive. When the fire was really heavy, Vern says to me, 'Rick, if I don't make it and you do, you'll tell Alice I loved her, won't you?' I told him not to talk nonsense. I said that wasn't going to happen, even though, deep down, I thought it might. If only one of us got home, I was sure at that point it would be him."

Tears rolled down Alice's cheeks, and Joan wiped her eyes. Only Tara seemed unmoved by the tale.

"Well, he kept after me, so I finally said sure. Of course I would do that for him, and he said he'd go see my mother if I didn't make it home. I was hurt bad. Couldn't walk. He stayed right beside me and gave me water. Tried to stop the bleeding. But snipers got behind us. Vern took a bullet in the back. Hit his lung, I guess. I could see that he wouldn't live. I honestly thought he and I would die there together."

They all sat in silence for a moment.

"But help came," he said. "Those North Dakota boys are tough. They drove the Japanese away. Vern was just about done in. The last thing he did was reach into his pocket for your picture." He looked over at Alice, his face taut, as though about to crumble. "He held it over his heart. And he died then, before the medic could get to us. When I reached to get your picture, I touched his dog tags. All of a sudden it hit me—Vern was dead, but I would go on with the fighting and wondering if I'd be arrested when I got home."

He paused for a moment, and Sarah wondered if he could continue. After a moment, he nodded as though resolved to finish the tale. "It happened so fast, I could hardly believe later that I'd done it. I whipped off my dog tags and switched them with Vern's." He smiled wryly and shook his head. "I figure if I hadn't been wounded bad enough to be shipped right off to a hospital, someone would have found out, and I'd have been … " He looked up as if suddenly aware of the women watching him. "I was plenty scared. When they came to us and saw Vern was dead, they started to give me first aid. They asked my name and I said 'Pickett.' They asked for my serial number, and that's when it hit me hard. I didn't have his number memorized. So I just played up the pain, like I couldn't concentrate enough to get it out. They looked at my tags—Vern's tags—and that was it. I couldn't go back after that. I was Vern Pickett."

"But ..." Joan stared at him, with a hurt expression. "But your family! Your poor mother."

He nodded. "They were informed that I died that day on Guadalcanal."

"Didn't you ever tell them?"

He sighed and shook his head. "If I did, it would have gotten out what I'd done. Then what? I didn't like what I'd done, but I couldn't see a way to change it after that moment when the medics came. I always regretted not being able to go back to my family. But the way I saw it, it could have been either one of us out there that day. It was pure dumb luck that I lived instead of dying out there with Vern."

"Oh my," said Alice. "It's like something out of one of my books. Only I don't think I'd have thought of that. Perhaps in a medieval setting ... "

Vern looked over at Tara. "Look, Miss ... Miss Giles, is it?"

"Yes." Tara's face was blank.

"I know I did wrong. But all these years—and it's a lot longer than your lifetime—it's been eating away at me. Yes, I took Vern's name. It was a chance for me to start fresh, to have a clean record and a new life. I made up my mind when I was discharged with Vern's papers that I would make a go of it. I'd earn an honest living. I wouldn't do anything that he couldn't have been proud of. I've lived a simple life, but I never stole again, and so far as I know, I've never broken another law. You ask my grandson, and he'll tell you. I don't cheat on my taxes. I don't even drive over the speed limit, or I didn't when I could still drive."

"But didn't your family know, when they got the wrong remains?" Joan asked.

"I don't know. I figured it must have been closed casket by the time they shipped the bodies home. I just don't know about that stuff. And I didn't try to find out."

Joan nodded soberly. "And when you got out of the hospital, what then?"

"I was absorbed into another platoon in the Massachusetts regiment, and eventually I mustered out."

"I kept writing to you," Alice said. "I mean Vern. Even when I hadn't heard for months, I kept writing for a long time."

He gritted his teeth. "Those days were bad—the days when I got your letters. A couple of them caught up with me while I was in the hospital. For a while I was too drugged up to read them, but after they decided I could keep my leg and it finally began to heal, there they were, waiting to be read. I realized then what I'd done, and how many people would be hurt. You deserved to know that the man you loved was dead, but I couldn't tell you that, because then I'd be discovered. And if I wrote to you as Vern, you'd know it wasn't his handwriting. So I never wrote back. I didn't know what else to do."

"But when you were discharged from the army," Sarah said, trying to puzzle it out, "didn't you *ever* contact your family?"

"No." He cleared his throat. "You have to understand, Sarah, my father didn't care about me. I didn't think much of myself, either. I suppose my mother did care on some level, but she had seven other kids to think about. And they'd been told I was dead. If I showed up, I couldn't just pick up my life as Richard Carini. Besides, maybe being arrested for that robbery and possible murder, I probably would have had the federal government after me. I'd been drawing Vern's pay and receiving benefits in his name. And they would have charged Richard Carini with going AWOL and a ton of other things more serious."

"They could charge a dead man—I mean, an officially dead man—with that?" Alice asked.

"I think it's a crime to fake your own death. At least if you gain by it or avoid punishment for another crime." He stared at the carpet. "I guess I am a criminal, one way or another."

"So what did you do after the war?" Joan asked.

He shrugged. "I bummed around for a while. I knew I had to stay away from my hometown. I took jobs here and there. But my promise to Vern weighed on me. Finally, in the fall of 1946, I went to Concord. Vern's town. I didn't tell anyone there who I was—either name. But I discovered some things by chatting with the residents." He looked at Alice. "I learned that you had married someone else. That was a big relief to me. It let me off the hook in a sense, because I thought you weren't still grieving for Vern."

Alice nodded. "I've always had a sorrow in my heart, wondering what became of him. But I learned from Mrs.

Pickett that he'd been wounded. I thought he'd come home, but he didn't. I kept writing letters. Then his mother died. I still didn't hear anything. I decided he didn't care enough about me to write or come back to me, and so I put that chapter of my life aside."

Joan reached over and patted her hand.

"It was difficult," Alice said. "But I moved on. For a while, I was quite happy. When my husband died, I was back in despair again—but that's another story. Let's hear the rest of yours." She nodded firmly at him.

"Well, I decided it was best for me to get out of Concord before I said too much. I didn't want word to get around that someone was asking questions about Vern. Anything that would draw attention to him would be bad for me. So I drove west, thinking I'd go as far as I could and find a place not near Concord or Vern's sister in Arizona or my own people in Illinois. Idaho, maybe. Someplace like that."

They all watched him expectantly.

"And?" Joan asked.

He chuckled. "My heap broke down in Pittsfield, a few miles from here. I've lived there ever since. Vern had wanted to prove himself to be a trustworthy, hardworking man, and I decided to do the same. I found that any small town was as good as another, if you worked hard and kept your mouth shut. And Pittsfield is a good town. I met a nice young lady, got married, had a family. I've had a pretty good life, all considered. I don't know if it's as good a life as Vern would have made if he'd lived, but—well, here I am."

He sat back in his chair and exhaled.

Sarah's mind raced. Was Vern's marriage legal, since he'd entered it under a false name? Better not to bring up things like that now, but she would ask Jason later. Her fingers itched for a pen and paper to write down all her questions, but she made herself sit still.

"What about Vern's sister Nora?" Alice asked.

"Apparently Vern and Nora weren't that close before the war. I managed to find an excuse every time she suggested getting together. I send her a card at Christmas, and once in a while she sends a letter. I tell her how my family's doing. But we've never met. She thinks I'm her brother. She's pretty old now—and she's in a nursing home down there in Arizona."

"So you continue to lie to her, year after year," Tara said.

At her bitter comment, Vern drew in a shaky breath and met her gaze. "Yeah, that about sums it up."

"What will you do now, Richard?" Alice asked.

He hesitated, then looked toward Sarah. "While your son was driving me over here, he told me he's a lawyer. He seems like a nice young man."

Sarah smiled. "I think so."

Vern nodded and turned back to Alice. "The first thing I'll do is tell my grandson Scott. That's going to be hard, but Scotty's got some of the old Carini grit in him, even though he doesn't know it. We'll get through it. And then I think I'll give Jason Hart a call and see if I can talk over the legal implications with him."

"I think that sounds like a good plan," Sarah said. "Jason will be happy to help. Now, friends, I believe it's time for lunch."

An hour later, as they all lingered at the dining room table over their pie and coffee, Sarah smiled across the table at Vern. She was proud of him for telling the truth at last, although it had been painful and he had a lot of work ahead of him.

There's something I still can't wrap my head around," Joan said. "Did your wife know who you really were?"

Vern looked down at his plate. "No. I spent a lot of time wrangling with whether or not to tell her. But I didn't before we got married, and afterward, I figured it would do more harm than good to tell her."

Alice smiled. "You can't undo the past. I don't know why you waited so long to confess, but I figure you told us your secret today because you wanted to make things right."

"That's true," Vern said. "I wanted to keep my promise and put an end to your wondering. But I wanted to stop my deceit too. It's bothered me all this time. I don't suppose things can ever be really right again. I mean ... like you said, we can't go back and undo it. Most of the people who would have cared are gone now."

"That's right." Sarah laid her hand lightly on Vern's shoulder. "Your parents and your wife and ... oh, it boggles the mind to even think about it! All the people who knew the real Vern are dead, too, except Nora and Alice and—"

"And me," Joan said. "Don't forget me. I suppose there are a few other people left in Concord. But the important thing is what you do from here. You're doing the right thing. It's going to be tough, but it's going to be all right."

"That's right," Alice murmured.

Sarah stood, and everyone looked her way. "Vern, I'm not sure this is the right time, but I have a gift for you."

"For me?"

"Yes. Scott asked me to make it for you, and he and McKenna helped make it happen. If you'll excuse me a moment, I'll get it for you." She went to the sewing room and returned with the protective plastic bag.

"Oh my. That's quite the gift," Vern said. "Should I take a peek now?"

"You can if you like." Sarah loosened the tie on the bag and set the bundle on his lap.

Vern worked the bag back off the folded quilt. "Look at that. You made this, didn't you?"

"Yes, I did. Oops, careful." Sarah reached to rescue the pillow sham before it could fall to the floor. "This will fit over your extra pillow and match the quilt."

"I . . ." Vern's eyes looked a bit misty as he gazed down at the quilt. "I don't know what to say. But . . . thank you."

Sarah smiled. "You're welcome."

Vern turned to Alice. "She made one like this for her dad. I didn't mean—"

Sarah waved one hand. "You didn't hint or anything. Scott thought it would be a wonderful gift for you and I agree." She pointed to one of the plaid squares. "As I said, I got help from Scott and McKenna. Do you recognize that?"

"That's my old shirt, isn't it?" He laughed. "I think I've seen this one before too. You're very creative."

"Thanks," Sarah said. "I hope you'll enjoy it. I'll set it in the other room for now, shall I?"

When she returned to the dining room, the others were chatting, and even Tara seemed amiable as she spoke to Vern.

"Marjory—" Tara stopped and smiled. "I suppose I'd better get used to calling you Alice now, like everyone else."

Alice returned her smile. "I'm just Alice today. What were you going to say, dear?"

"I wondered if you're getting tired?"

"Me? Tired? I haven't felt this energized in years. Although I admit I'll probably sleep soundly tonight."

"I wondered when your next book will come out," Joan said.

"Do you know, I've decided to write a new story. Oh, I have another novel coming out in June, but that one's all written. I wondered for a while if it would be my last. I'm not getting any younger, you know—am I, Joan?"

She and her friend laughed. Joan said, "My dear Alice, you'll always be young in spirit."

"Thank you. Anyway, I think I may write a sequel to *Before the Storm*. Now that I know what really happened, I think I'll write the story of my characters the way I always wished I could have lived. The heroine will marry her child-hood sweetheart and live happily ever after."

"I'm surprised at you," Joan said. "It will be a very boring book if you don't put some conflict in it."

They all chuckled, but Alice waved one hand through the air. "Don't you worry. There'll be plenty of conflict." She gazed pointedly across at Vern. "Richard Carini, there's something I'd like to say to you in front of all these people."

"Uh … what's that?" He gritted his teeth as though ex-pecting a tirade.

"Knowing the real Vern loved me to the end is much more comforting than thinking he just got tired of me and stopped writing."

"Never," Vern said. "I apologize again for the pain I caused you over the years by not telling you what really happened to Vern—or that he died a hero. You deserved to know that, and I was a heel for not making sure you knew."

Alice hesitated, then said, "Well, yes, you were. But I for-give you anyway."

Vern smiled wistfully as the others laughed. "You know, Vern really was a hero. They pinned a medal on me that should have gone to Vern." He looked over at Sarah. "Sarah, where's my coat?"

"In the hall closet. Would you like me to get it?"

"In the left-hand pocket. Do you mind?"

Sarah hurried out to the entry and opened the closet. She found Vern's jacket, and in the pocket was a hard jeweler's case. She took it back to the dining room and held it out to Vern.

"Take it over to Alice," he said. "She should have had it, years ago. Oh, I suppose they'd have sent it to Nora if they'd had the right man, but I think Alice should have it."

Alice took the case from Sarah and fumbled to open it. Inside was a Purple Heart medal on a ribbon.

"I've felt guilty having that all this time," Vern said. "My own family got the medal awarded to Richard Carini posthumously—every man in the squad got one. But this is Vern's medal, and... if you'd take it...?"

"I'd be honored," Alice said. She passed the case to Joan, who gazed down at the medal with tears in her eyes and then passed it to Tara. Alice smiled, looking around the table. "This is not a time for mourning, dear friends. Vern Pickett was a friend and a hero, and I loved him. He couldn't do the things he wanted to do, he but did one last thing—he brought us all together. Let's celebrate this reunion."

"I agree," Joan said, picking up her teacup. "Let's toast the finding of old friends." She raised the cup in Alice's direction.

"Yes," said Alice, looking over at Vern. "And new ones. Welcome, Richard."

ABOUT THE AUTHOR

Susan Page Davis has published more than thirty novels in the historical romance, suspense, mystery, and romance genres. She's a past winner of the American Christian Fiction Writers' Book of the Year Contest (Carol Award), and a two-time winner of the Inspirational Readers' Choice Contest. A Maine native, she now resides in Kentucky with her husband, Jim, who is a freelance book editor. The two youngest of their six children also live at home. The Davises have six brilliant and adorable grandchildren and an array of pets: a black Labrador retriever cross, a calico cat, and a Tennessee Walker colt. Susan loves to read and do needlework, logic puzzles, and genealogy research. She's a long time home schooler and former schoolteacher. Visit Susan at her Website: www.susanpagedavis.com

THREADS OF TRUTH

BY KRISTIN ECKHARDT

 CHAPTER ONE

Sarah Hart leaned forward, squinting to see through the tiny shards of ice clinging to the windshield. She hated driving in icy conditions, especially in unfamiliar territory. Her gloved hands gripped the steering wheel as she drove along the dark country road, looking for some signs of life. She hadn't seen a house for miles, not one place she could stop and ask for directions.

Her twin granddaughters both dozed in the car, Audrey in the bucket seat beside her and Amy in the back, her long legs stretched across the seat. Sarah had asked them to go to Hartford with her after she'd been invited to give a workshop at the annual Connecticut Quilt Makers Conference. They were more excited about spending the weekend in a hotel than about attending the conference, but she would make sure they had fun.

The plan had been to leave Friday evening after Amy's junior high basketball game and arrive at the Red Clover Inn by nine o'clock. Unfortunately, Sarah hadn't planned on encountering an ice storm or getting lost on the way to the historic country inn. The inn was located on the outskirts of Hartford and the map was hard to follow. She'd tried calling the inn for directions, but her cell phone kept cutting out.

Icy sleet and ominous darkness filled the night sky. Sarah tried not to be afraid but it wasn't easy, especially since she still wasn't sure if they were heading in the right direction. She could see the city lights of Hartford glowing on the horizon. The moment she thought she should circle back, her headlights flashed on a white wooden sign with RED CLOVER INN painted in bright red letters.

Finally!

She tried to depress the brakes gently, but the tires skidded on the slick asphalt before the Grand Prix finally came to a stop. She shifted the car into reverse, carefully backed up, and turned into the private driveway that led to the inn.

"Are we there yet?" Amy's groggy voice asked from the backseat. She still wore her royal blue and white jersey under her coat along with a pair of blue flannel pants.

"Yes, we finally made it," Sarah replied as Audrey began to stir beside her. Relief flowed through her as she breathed a silent prayer. *Thank you, Lord, for bringing us here safely.*

Through the towering blue spruce trees lining the long driveway, Sarah glimpsed the shadowy outline of the inn ahead of her. She had heard about the secluded inn from

Spencer Hewitt, Maple Hill's librarian, and had been intrigued by its history. According to Spencer, the English-style manor house had been built in 1890, during the height of the Gilded Age, and still retained most of its original décor and period furniture.

Audrey yawned, tugging the hood of her coat back to reveal her long blonde hair in a messy ponytail. She leaned forward for a better view of the inn, her blue eyes surveying the icy landscape with surprise. "This is where we're staying?"

"It sure is," Sarah replied.

The two-story inn constructed of russet sandstone loomed in front of them. The double chimneys stretched like two long arms into the turbulent gray clouds above. Leafless shrubs hugged the front of the house, their naked branches shivering in the wind.

She pulled alongside a line of cars and switched off the engine. The rattle of sleet grew louder. "Let's grab our bags and get inside," Sarah told them. "Just be careful in case the sidewalk is slippery."

Audrey slung her backpack over one shoulder and popped open her car door, admitting a frigid blast of air. "Wow, it's freezing out here!"

Sarah reached for her overnight bag. The twins were almost at the front entrance by the time she locked the car and headed down the sidewalk. She bent her head to shield her face from the wind, the sleet stinging her face. The twins waited for her by the solid oak door, Amy tracing the iron scrollwork over the frosted glass panel with one gloved finger. Sarah turned the brass doorknob and walked inside the grand, two-story foyer, the girls close on her heels.

The warmth of the inn melted away the tension that had gripped Sarah during the long trip. To the left of the foyer was a large parlor filled with antique furniture, beautiful Persian rugs, and a roaring blaze in the stone fireplace. Heavy gold drapes hung from the top of the windows to the polished wood floor. Sarah peeked in and saw that the parlor opened into a small library with mahogany bookcases reaching as high as the twelve-foot ceiling. A cozy window seat adorned the alcove, full of plush red cushions and striped pillows. It looked like the perfect place to lose oneself in a book. The girls looked into the dining room to the right of the foyer; a circular staircase wound above them with the front desk of the inn nestled beneath it. So absorbed with her surroundings, it took Sarah a moment to notice a short, burly man standing behind the green marble counter wearing an oatmeal-colored sweater and chatting with another man on the other side of the counter.

Behind the front desk was a wide hallway and Sarah could just glimpse a large kitchen on the left. On the right side of the hallway was one door and it was closed. The innkeeper looked up when he saw Sarah and the girls approaching. "Welcome to the Red Clover Inn." He sported a thatch of thick white hair, although he looked no older than forty-five.

The other man gave them a brief glance and headed for the stairs. "We'll talk later?"

"Sure," the innkeeper replied and turned his gaze back to Sarah and the girls. "You must be Mrs. Hart." He rounded the counter and reached out to shake her hand. "I'm Patrick Maguire. I believe we talked on the phone when you reserved your rooms."

"We did," Sarah affirmed, remembering her conversation. The man was rather chatty on the phone. "It's nice to meet you, Mr. Maguire."

A dimple flashed in his cheek. "I insist you call me Patrick." He turned to the twins. "And these must be your two lovely granddaughters."

"This is Audrey," Sarah said, placing one hand on Audrey's shoulder, "and her sister Amy."

Patrick's green eyes twinkled. "I hope you two are the adventurous type. I picked out a special room for you."

"What kind of room?" Audrey asked.

His smile widened. "You'll see." Then he turned back toward the front desk. "But first we need to get the three of you checked in. I was beginning to wonder if you were going to show up tonight."

"So was I." Sarah set her purse on the marble counter, the surface as smooth as glass. It was one of the few pieces of modern furniture in the room. "I tried to phone you, but my call wouldn't go through."

"Cell phone reception is pretty spotty around these parts. I've got a landline phone here," he said, nodding toward the cordless unit on his desk, "if you need to make a call."

"Actually, we do." She turned to the girls. "Why don't you call your folks and let them know we arrived?"

"Talk as long as you like," Patrick told them, reaching for the can of soda on the counter. He handed the receiver to Audrey and set the guest registry in front of Sarah.

"I want to call," Amy said, grabbing for the phone.

Audrey pulled it out of her grasp. "He gave it to me."

"Girls," Sarah said. "Just take turns. Audrey, you talk first and then give the phone to your sister."

She turned back to the counter. "Now, where would you like me to sign?"

"Right here," he said, his finger weaving over the registry before he planted it on a blank line below the name Dorothy Ogden. "My printer's out of ink or I'd print out a copy of your registration. I'll make sure you get a receipt before you check out."

"That's fine."

"Would you like a wake-up call for breakfast or do you want to sleep in?"

"We need to leave for Hartford by eight." She could hear Audrey telling her parents about their trip while Amy hovered over her, begging for her turn. "What time is breakfast?"

"Nine o'clock," Patrick said and took another swig of his soda. "But I always have coffee, juice, and rolls set out for the early birds."

"That sounds perfect." Sarah capped the pen. "I just hope the weather is decent."

"Should be sunny and clear. We're just catching the very edge of a storm front right now, but according to the latest weather report it's moving to the north."

Sarah breathed a sigh of relief. "That's good to hear."

A lanky young man emerged from the back carrying a yellow plastic sack.

"Where have you been?" Patrick said to him.

The young man swept the curtain of shaggy brown hair off his forehead and held up the sack in his hand. "I went to find salt for the front walk like you told me."

"That was almost half an hour ago," Patrick said and strained out a smile as he turned back to Sarah. "Would you take these ladies' suitcases up to their rooms?"

"Okay." He set the sack on the floor.

"Don't put it there," Patrick said. "If the salt leaks out it could ruin the floor. Put it back in the pantry first."

As the young man picked up the sack and headed for the kitchen, Sarah heard him muttering something unintelligible under his breath.

"This way, ladies." Patrick rounded the counter and escorted them to the stately mahogany staircase.

Sarah glanced around the main floor as they walked, impressed by the arched doorways, intricately carved woodwork, and lofty plank ceiling. "This is a beautiful building. I feel like I've stepped back into the past."

"Thank you," Patrick replied. "It takes a lot of work to maintain a place like this, but I think it's worth it."

Sarah agreed. Everything was pristine and well polished, including the brass chandeliers that lit their path up the staircase and dotted the hallway ceiling on the second floor.

When they reached the top of the stairs, they walked past several closed doors, their footsteps silent on the plush floral hall runner. Sarah was surprised they didn't encounter any other guests and then glanced at her watch and saw that it was almost eleven o'clock.

"Here we are, girls," Patrick announced as he opened the door in front of them. "This is your room for the weekend."

Amy and Audrey's eyes widened when they saw the huge bearskin rug in the center of the floor. The black bear's head was still attached and the mouth was open wide enough to reveal razor sharp teeth.

"Is that real?" Audrey gasped, pointing to the bearskin rug.

Patrick chuckled. "No, it's just a really good imitation. I found it in the attic when I bought the place and knew I had to use it in one of the guest rooms. I had a lot of fun decorating this one.

Sarah almost giggled at the awe-struck expressions on the girls' faces. She glanced around the rest of the room, taking in the rustic log furniture, forest green drapes, and king-size bed.

"This is pretty cool." Amy walked into the room and shrugged off her coat. Then she pulled her cell phone out of her pocket and began to take pictures of the room.

"I'm glad you like it," Patrick said and turned to Audrey. "How about you?"

"It's nice, I guess." Audrey looked down at the rug. "I'm just glad that wasn't a real bear."

"No dangerous animals here. And even if there were, your grandma's room is right through here."

Sarah followed him through the connecting door while the twins stayed behind to explore their room. After seeing that bearskin rug, Sarah was ready for anything. But when Patrick opened the door to her room, she was pleasantly surprised by the tranquil, Victorian atmosphere.

"How lovely." Sarah walked over to the rosewood sleigh bed. She ran one hand along the faded green, blue, and yellow patches of the antique quilt. "You don't see this Grandmother's Puzzle pattern very often."

"I thought it was fitting since you're traveling with your granddaughters." He pointed to a sepia portrait on the wall. "That's my grandmother, Maeve Ryan Maguire. She immigrated here from Ireland when she was twelve years old, but she never lost her Irish brogue nor her love for the old country."

"She must have been very special if you designed a room in her honor."

Patrick didn't reply, his eyelids drooping as if he were dozing off. Then he popped them open again, his gaze unfocused. He didn't smell like alcohol, but that could not have been plain old cola he was drinking.

"She was special," Patrick said after the awkward pause. "She helped raise me after my mum died and never put up with any nonsense."

Sarah could hear the love in his voice. She walked over to study the portrait. The woman's expression was very somber, like most photographic subjects of that era, but Sarah could see a sparkle in her eyes and the strong set of her shoulders. "What a wonderful portrait for you to remember her by."

"It is," Patrick agreed. "Most of the furniture in this room belonged to her, and she made those lace curtains. I wanted to put all of her things to good use, since she taught me how to make do with what I have."

A knock at the door made them both turn. "That must be Levi," Patrick said, walking over to open it.

The young man walked into the room carrying a suitcase in each hand and one tucked under his arm. "Where would you like me to set these, ma'am?"

"Just put them down anywhere," Sarah said as the girls walked through the connecting door into her room.

Levi set the suitcases by the bed, then glanced over at Patrick. "Anything else you want me to do before I clock out for the night?"

"Wait for me downstairs," Patrick told him.

Sarah reached into her purse and retrieved a couple of dollar bills for Levi. "Thank you for bringing up our bags."

"You're welcome." Levi took the money from her before turning and walking out the door, leaving it open behind him.

Patrick turned back to Sarah, his smile in place once more. "Now, as you can see, each room has a private bath and they're fully stocked with towels and toiletries. There are extra blankets in the closet and you'll find the television remote control in the drawer of your nightstand. We only have televisions in the guest rooms, there are none downstairs."

"Do you have Internet?" Audrey asked him.

"Sorry," Patrick said, "we like to keep things simple around here."

"I think we can survive off-line for one weekend," Sarah said.

"Is there anything else you need?" he asked. "Of course, you're welcome to spend time in the parlor if you're not ready for bed yet."

"No, we're fine." Sarah told him. "We have a big day tomorrow—"

"Maguire," a voice said from the hallway.

Patrick turned around as the man who had been talking with him in the lobby appeared in the open doorway. "Yes?"

"Finish our conversation?" the man asked, then noticed Sarah. He tilted his head toward the hallway in a not-so-subtle manner. "In private?"

"Sure," Patrick said to him.

The man gave him a brisk nod. "I'll be downstairs."

Patrick moved to follow him. "See you in the morning, ladies."

"Good night." Sarah closed the door behind him, wondering if the man who was so rude was an employee or a guest. When she turned around she saw both girls frowning at her. "What's wrong?"

"We don't have to go to bed yet, do we?" Amy asked.

"It *is* pretty late," Sarah replied.

"But it's Friday night," Audrey said. "We always get to stay up later on the weekend. Please, Grandma."

"Please," echoed Amy.

Despite their long faces, Sarah had fought these bedtime battles with her own children and knew a tired child when she saw one. At the moment, there were two of them standing in front of her.

"As I told Mr. Maguire, we have a long day ahead of us tomorrow." She walked over to the girls and placed an arm around each one. "You two put on your pajamas and get in bed. You can read or watch television until you fall asleep."

Audrey looked like she wanted to argue, but Amy picked up her suitcase. "Let's just go to bed, Audrey. We don't have to fall asleep yet."

"Good night, girls," Sarah said as she watched them walk back to their room.

"Good night," they mumbled.

Sarah slipped off her wool coat and set her purse on the pink marble-topped dresser. She caught a glimpse of herself in the oval mirror, grimaced, and reached into her purse for a comb.

After she had tamed her graying blonde hair, she opened the top drawer of the dresser to place her comb inside and found an old Bible nestled there. She smoothed her fingers over the white leather cover, then carefully opened it.

After turning a few blank pages, she found the name Maeve Ryan inscribed in spidery black ink, along with a verse from Matthew 6:21: "For where your treasure is, there your heart will be also."

She turned the next page and found a family tree spanning both pages. Sarah carefully traced the branches, finding Maeve's name below the names of her parents and grandparents. She'd been born in 1920 and married a man named John Maguire in 1938. They'd had one child, Shawn Maguire, born in 1942. Shawn had married Mary Kerr and their son, Patrick Shawn Maguire, had been born in 1966.

But that wasn't the only bit of information she gleaned from Maeve's Bible. Patrick had married a woman named Hope Weaver in 1988, although Sarah hadn't seen a wedding ring on his left hand and there was no sign of family at the inn. There were no new branches added to the family tree after that, although someone had scribbled in Maeve's death in 1988. She assumed Patrick had written it, since he seemed so close to his grandmother.

She paged through the Bible, noting that Maeve had underlined several passages. It had obviously been well read and well loved. She placed the Bible back in the drawer and closed it, envying Patrick for owning such a precious treasure from his grandmother.

The house creaked and moaned under the force of the winter wind. She walked over to the window and pulled back the Irish lace curtain, only to find the windowpane covered with a sheet of ice, distorting the shape of the trees outside. She shivered as frigid air slipped through tiny cracks in the old window. Sarah let the curtain fall from her hand and walked over to her suitcase to retrieve a cardigan. That's when she realized she had left her laptop computer in the car. She needed it to put the finishing touches on tomorrow's workshop presentation.

With a groan, Sarah donned her coat once more, walked over to the twins' room, and stuck her head inside. Amy lay in bed reading while Audrey sat on the bed next to her looking at pictures on her cell phone.

"I need to run down to the car for a minute, girls. I'll be right back."

"Okay," Amy said, not looking up from her book. "We'll be here."

"We're still wide awake," Audrey added, her words ending on a yawn.

Sarah smiled to herself as she walked downstairs, but her smile faded when she reached the front door. Wind rattled the brass doorknob, as if trying to gain entrance. The last thing she wanted to do was go out in that ice storm again.

She readied herself and opened the door to a flurry of tiny ice pellets. She stepped carefully out onto the front step, the pavement slick under her feet. She grasped the handrail, also covered with ice, and made her way gingerly down the steps.

The treacherous walk to her car seemed to take ages, the wind constantly trying to push her back. She leaned forward, head down, the inky darkness and driving sleet making it difficult to see more than a few feet in front of her.

When she finally reached the car, she inserted the key into the trunk and struggled to open it. Ice had filled the crevices, making it necessary for her to yank on the trunk lid several times before the icy bond finally broke.

She reached inside the trunk and pulled out her laptop case, eager to return to the inn. The wind was at her back now, making her journey back to the inn a little less arduous.

Sarah savored the warmth as she walked through the front door, her body shivering. Then she heard something odd. She paused, her ears perked, before she realized the noise was the sound of a scuffle coming from the parlor.

She walked over in time to see a man hurrying out of the room. He had his back to her, so she couldn't see his face. He favored his right leg as he walked and soon disappeared into the shadows.

She turned toward the parlor and saw Patrick standing with one hand braced against the fireplace mantle.

"Patrick, are you okay?" she asked.

"Oh, I'm fine. Just a slight…disagreement." Patrick rubbed one hand over his eyes. "It's the plight of an innkeeper to deal with demanding guests."

She sensed he was glossing over the incident and could see him struggling to retain both his balance and his composure. "Are you sure you're all right? Can I get you anything?"

"No, no, I'm fine," he said with a dismissive wave. "I usually try to be as accommodating as possible, but some people just can't be satisfied. I'm sorry if we disturbed you."

"Not at all," she assured him, still uneasy about what she'd just witnessed. "I just had to get my laptop out of my car."

He nodded, but didn't seem to be listening. He closed his eyes and leaned his head back against the stone chimney.

"Well, good night again," she said, heading toward the stairs.

"Good night."

Sarah returned to her room and checked on the girls, who were both fast asleep. She tucked the bed's vintage quilt around their shoulders, kissed each girl on the forehead, and returned to her own room.

For the next hour, she struggled to stay awake while she worked on the laptop. She even nodded off once, until the sound of a door slamming somewhere below woke her up again.

When she finally climbed into bed, she welcomed the heavy quilt and coverlet, still feeling slightly chilled from her trip to the car. Her eyes drifted shut as soon as her head hit the pillow and she fell into a dreamless sleep.

The muffled sounds of a baby crying awakened her in the middle of the night. She turned over and glanced at the clock on the antique nightstand.

Three o'clock.

She groaned, turned over, and closed her eyes again. Sleet continued to batter the windowpane and the howling wind competed with the baby's cries. She'd always had trouble sleeping in a strange bed and the creaks and groans of the unfamiliar house made it difficult for her to fall back to sleep.

Thirty minutes later, the wind calmed and the baby finally stopped crying. Sarah closed her eyes again, knowing she had precious few hours of slumber left. After several moments of blessed silence, she finally drifted off into a deep sleep.

The next thing she knew, a bloodcurdling scream ripped through the air.

A NOTE FROM THE EDITORS

Guideposts, a nonprofit organization, touches millions of lives every day through products and services that inspire, encourage and uplift. Our magazines, books, prayer network and outreach programs help people connect their faith-filled values to their daily lives. To learn more, visit www.guideposts. com or www.guidepostsfoundation.org.